The Life and Times of
DAFFODIL MULLIGAN

The Life and Times of
DAFFODIL MULLIGAN

Maggie Redding

BRILLIANCE BOOKS

First published by Brilliance Books 1984

Brilliance Books 14 Clerkenwell Green London EC1

ISBN 0 946189 16 1 (paperback)
ISBN 0 946189 21 8 (hardback)

Typeset by MC Typeset Chatham Kent
Printed and bound in Great Britain by
Nene Litho and Woolnough Bookbinding both of
Wellingborough, Northants.

For Sylvia with love,
and Martha, with thanks

CHAPTER 1

In our family there have been many theories put forward to explain why I am such a problem, but I have one of my own which I dare not tell the others.

My sister and I are very different to look at – and in other ways, too. But it is the sight of us side by side even now that amazes people. She is tall, slim, dark with a slightly olive complexion that earned her the nickname 'Gypsy Lena' as a child. I am, and always have been, big, blonde, pink and white, with fat legs and very clean and tidy.

Friends of my mother, or acquaintances – I never knew how well she knew these people – would often stop her in the street and comment on how dark my sister was, and how fair I was.

One particular woman, surely an acquaintance, went a bit further than all the others. 'Isn't it strange,' she said, 'that your daughters are so different, the eldest so fair, not a bit like her father, and the youngest so dark.'

My mother, who is very sensitive about anything remotely connected with sex, took a deep breath; then she threw back her head, flaring her nostrils and gripping the pram, and said in loud nearly-cultured tones acquired in service with minor nobility: 'Yes, I had her after I was married.'

The pram rocked violently and mother stormed away, me

clutching the pram handle and having to run to keep up with her, my fat legs wobbling.

I could claim that a myth grew up in the locality that I was a bastard and that it ruined my life and caused me to be a problem. But, no, it didn't because no one ever tackled my mother concerning my sister and me with such gross lack of tact again. Perhaps in recounting the incident the woman realized the depth of my mother's wit and sarcasm and warning passed round the neighbourhood. I don't know. That is the sad part of making witty and sarcastic remarks. One doesn't usually see the dawning of truth, not if it is really good wit and really shrivelling sarcasm. Whatever happened, people always make a comment like: 'Isn't your eldest daughter like you! And your youngest is so like your husband!' which pleases Mother no end.

Perhaps it was being my mother's clone that made me such a problem. 'You're so like I was at your age Daffodil,' was certainly a very powerful way of controlling me. And it worked for some years.

Buster was about six weeks old when Lena and I first saw him. We had been sent to Grandma's for three months. I have never been given a good reason why but I suspect it was so we should not see mother's big belly before the baby was born and how flat it was after, in case we put two and two together. At six years old I believed implicitly in the stork.

I think it was the day after we came back from Grandma's that Buster had his vaccination against smallpox. Lena and I were of course fascinated by all this. Mother left us by the pram of the now quietened baby while she saw the doctor out of the house. Buster was lying there, half-naked, without his nappy because the vaccination had been done on his leg. This meant his willie was exposed. I had never, in my six years, seen one before. This was the moment of revelation – boys and girls were different. I had no need to ask. I knew. It was not, after all, that men had short hair and women had long hair. Buster had fairly long dark curls. It was to do with this thing that wiggled a bit as he kicked his fat legs.

Lena and I looked at each other.

'Touch it,' I said.

'No, you,' she said.

So, having confirmed that the curiosity was not just a quirk of mine, I put my hand out and touched it.

'Oh! You mustn't do that.' said Mother's voice behind me. 'You must never touch that.'

'Why not?' I asked, pulling back, amazed. I got no answer.

There are only two reasons for not touching something – it's either dirty or sacred. Which was this?

My conclusion, some years after this incident, was that my mother would have liked to have been the victim of unbridled sexual passions, but being a good Catholic girl and the daughter of parents who were born during Victorian times, she must bridle those passions most severely. This was my hypothesis. This, I concluded, was the cause of my problems or rather, my being seen as a problem.

CHAPTER 2

I spent three years from the age of three at a convent school. There I learned, through very progressive Montessori methods, to read, write, count, draw, sing and speak French and to think for myself – in some respect anyway. I also learned about religion, that is, Catholicism of a Jansenist variety, authoritarian, frightening, heretical. I learned about God, all-powerful, Adam and Eve, the devil, guardian angels.

All this was an outlet for my vivid imagination, or perhaps it was a stimulus for it. I loved my faith. I can remember my First Communion day vividly, especially the martyrdom of being the only girl not wearing white shoes and not having to mention it because we were poor and Mother had done her best. In summer, Lena and I would be packed off to Mass on Sunday while the parents and Buster stayed at home preparing the Sunday dinner. Knowing the commandments of the church about attending Mass on Sunday I was a bit worried about my parents' salvation, but on speaking to my mother about it was assured that she had a dispensation because Buster was so young. Thus content, I would relax and enjoy the ceremony, the mysteriousness of it, the colour, light, movement and smells of incense and flowers. Outside the sky was blue and the air quivering with heat and expectation.

At the convent, as well as on religion, they fed us on vegetables from their garden. One day, I collected my dinner on a blue-and-white willow pattern plate, sat down at my pink table and ate everything on it except the leeks. These were green and slimy and stank. I felt revolted. I could not eat them. I tried to return my plate.

'Daffodil, go back to your table and eat your leeks.'

I returned and looked at the horrid mess on my plate and started to play with it. I noticed that you could see through leeks if you spread them out in thin layers. I sat there spreading out the leeks until I could see the pattern of the plate through them. Then, when my teacher was not looking, I crept up to the pile of returned plates and tried to squeeze mine in half-way down the pile. I had some trouble. A big girl, who must have been all of eleven years old, came to my aid.

'What are you doing, Daffodil?'

'I'm trying to put my plate in there,' I said, with a sidelong glance at her.

'Give it to me,' she said. She saw the leeks, but said nothing. I went back to my table. The teacher came over to me.

'Daffodil, you did not eat up all your dinner.'

I said nothing.

'Why not, Daffodil?'

I stamped my foot. 'I don't like them. I don't want them. I'm going home.'

I got up and ran from the classroom to the cloakroom. I began putting my coat on. It was the practice in the school that pupils put on their coats and sat in the cloakroom to wait for their mothers to collect them. I knew I could not go out of school alone. At four, I was not so simple as to believe that putting on my coat and sitting in the cloakroom would summon my mother. I also knew that they did not know I knew this.

'What are you doing, Daffodil?' asked the worried teacher.

'I am putting on my coat. I will wait for my mummy to come and taken me home. I won't eat my dinner.' I was defiant and strong.

The teacher went out, leaving the big girl in the cloakroom to talk to me.

'I'm going home. I don't want my dinner. My mummy will come and take me home.'

The teacher returned very quickly, another big girl at her side.

'Mother Hyacinth wants to see you.'

Mother Hyacinth was the headmistress. I should have been in awe. I rose fearlessly.

'Aren't you going to take your coat off?' the teacher asked.

'No,' I replied rebelliously. 'My mummy is coming to take me home.' I knew I had got them worried.

The big girl took my hand and led me upstairs to Mother Hyacinth's room. This took some time as I did not negotiate stairs very speedily. By the time I got to Mother Hyacinth's room, I had forgotten about the leeks and Mummy coming to fetch me.

Mother Hyacinth was very kind and explained to me gently that I must eat all my dinner and must not go home before home time.

'Give me your coat,' she said.

I obeyed, struggling out of it without her help. Suddenly I found myself lying face down across her lap and being slapped on the bottom. Just as suddenly, I was upright again and being led by the hand out of the room and downstairs again by Mother Hyacinth. On the way down the stairs, Mother Hyacinth taught me how to put one foot in front of the other instead of putting the same foot down on the next step all the time. I was returned to my classroom and given my pudding and was only vaguely able to connect the leeks, my threat to go home and the spanking. Mother Hyacinth and the teachers were not to know that at home I got spanked harder and shrieked at when I did something to displease my mother.

Auntie Rose was as different from Mother as it is possible for a sister to be. Warm, affectionate, indulgent, punishment to her was unthinkable. Throughout our childhood, Lena and I spent many happy holidays with her, Uncle Wack, cousin Ritchie and Grandma and Grandad. Holidays with Auntie Rose, as well as freedom, meant strong hot tea, runner beans from the garden and bought cake. We couldn't afford bought cake at home, so to us this was a real luxury.

Grandad had a big garden and the house overlooked the railway station. Early in the morning and late in the evening, Lena and I would stand on our bed in the ladies' satin petticoats that were our nighties – cast-offs from Auntie Rose – and watch the trains depart, listen to the announcements and worry about the pigeons let out of their baskets finding their way home again.

It was lovely. The freedom! We were allowed to play in the street. I borrowed Uncle Wack's old bone-shaker of a bike and rode round the streets with the local children. We would bag rides on the milk cart, were allowed to get dirty and to pick raspberries from the garden. Some days we would wash and change our dresses and Auntie Rose would make a great fuss of doing our hair and we would go 'up town'. She wanted to show us off. We were spoilt, too, unlike at home; Mother would never buy us Smarties or Wagon Wheels to eat in the street. And at weekends Uncle Wack would get the car ready, Auntie Rose would prepare an elaborate picnic of all things we didn't get at home and we would be taken to the hills, or the woods or mountains or the seaside. I learnt to love the countryside, to relate geography to the realities of the landscape, to identify birds, wild flowers, trees, rocks.

Our cousin, Ritchie, Auntie Rose's and Uncle Wack's son,

was the original *enfant terrible*. Was my mother pleased! He was cheeky, he was daring, defiant, always laughing. He did very poorly at school. My Mother was even more pleased because we all went to the grammar school.

Once when we slept in Grandma's bed, while she went to stay with Auntie June, Ritchie put caterpillars in it. I pulled back the sheets and saw them. Lena, being competitive, was already in bed, lying on them. I screamed, Lena screamed and Ritchie was chased by his mother round the house, down the garden and up the road – in his pyjamas. He stood taunting Auntie Rose on the opposite pavement.

'You can't catch me. Go on, then. Catch me.'

And, of course, she couldn't and we all ended up laughing.

When we were older, we were allowed to take Ritchie 'up town' on our own. This was great. It meant even more freedom. We would have money to spend on sweets and ice-creams, we could go on the swings, then round the cathedral where, being good Catholic children, and well versed in the history of the Reformation, we tickled the toes of all the effigies on the tombs dated after 1539. On hot summer days we would go down to the river and secretly paddle. This was forbidden because the currents were dangerous but we took care and Auntie Rose never found out.

Oddly enough, amidst all this freedom, even in adolescence, sex did not rear its ugly head on these holidays. It was only at home that I even bothered to think about it.

When the time came to go home, I always cried. The sun always shone on these holidays; our return home was always to rain – or so it seemed.

At six I was sent to an ordinary state primary school. Mill End School was totally different from the convent. No grass lawns and gardens, no interesting Montessori apparatus, no little pink-and-blue tables or clean lavatories indoors. This school had an asphalt playground, outside lavatories and some children from very poor families. I could tell who these were because they had no socks on, wore cotton dresses even in winter, had badly combed hair and snotty noses. I quickly became aware of the existence of a dirty kind of poverty and of a division of people into approved and not approved. Later I learned from my mother that the word 'common' covered dirtiness, poverty and usually what she perceived as a lack of morals.

Some children were acceptable and among those who passed Mother's test was Wendy, the girl who came to live next door but one. She was in my class at school, so we became very firm friends, periodically falling out and making it up a day or two later.

During one long, hot, lazy summer, Lena, Wendy and I began to play hospitals. Wendy and I both wanted to be nurses. The game began innocently enough, with the patient lying down in the grass and having all manner of concoctions – mainly water with rose petals floating in – poured over various innocent parts of each other's anatomy.

Then we discovered belly-buttons. That was quite fun, having a rose petal placed on it, then water dripped gently on to it from a spoon from a dolls' tea-set.

Sometimes, to get to belly-buttons, you had to pull knickers down slightly. If you pulled them down a bit more, there were even more interesting things on which to pour water, rose petals and tickle with grass stalks.

Once we discovered this, playing hospitals became an obsession and was spoken about in capital letters, unless of course we were talking to grown-ups.

'What have you been doing all evening?'

'Oh, just playing hospitals.'

But, earlier in the evening when we met at the bottom of our very long gardens, we would say excitedly, 'Let's Play Hospitals.' This, after the casual greetings and exchanges about someone's new sandals, cut finger, washed hair.

'Yes, all right. Can *they* see?' we would ask, kneeling down among the waist-high grass and weeds and gazing towards the windows of the row of terraced houses.

'No. Anyway, there's nothing wrong in playing hospitals.'

'Course not.'

'Bags I first,' one of us would say, claiming the right to be the first patient.

One day Wendy met us at the bottom of the garden. She looked slightly uneasy.

'We went up the town today,' I said.

'So did I,' said Lena.

Wendy ignored her.

'Did you get anything?'

'No,' I replied, wriggling, because I never got anything. 'Buster fell over.'

We stood around, as children do, unembarrassed by the silence or not having anything to say.

'Let's Play Hospitals,' I said.

'I can't,' Wendy answered unexpectedly. 'I'm not allowed. My mum said I mustn't. When I came out she said "Now don't get playing hospitals".'

I looked at her in disbelief. I thought she was telling lies. I had never *told* my mother we played hospitals and I had assumed she had not told hers. Besides, even if we had mentioned it, the mothers were not likely to know that our version was a bit rude. I guessed that Wendy herself felt that Playing Hospitals was naughty. Disappointment mixed with guilt agitated me.

'Let's play, – I looked about me wildly – 'going for a walk.'

It was easy to assume that Wendy was telling a lie because I told so many. They were not so much lies as fantasies, stories in my mind of how I wished life could be. We were very poor, but also very respectable as a family, and had certain ambitions. Even at seven years of age I had ambitions. I wanted to learn to swim, to ride a bicycle, to play the piano and to have ballet lessons.

When I was older I did teach myself to swim. We were a bit better off financially at that time and could afford nightly admission to the swimming pool. Eventually I learned to ride a bike and actually had a bike of my own, but when I was seven such luxuries were out of the question. Neither piano nor lessons could be afforded and I don't think either of my parents would have known where to find a piano or a piano teacher if they had had the money.

What really hurt was that so many of my friends went to the local dancing school. So frustrated was I that, with the help of Lena and Wendy, I invented something called 'steps'.

'We've got to hurry home tonight,' we'd say, 'we've got to go to "steps".'

And every Tuesday night, because we didn't want to be found out as liars, we stopped at the U-shaped tree along the sunken lane that was our route home from school, jigged about a bit and tried to contrive some weird footwork to confound and impress our friends.

Such fantasies I had about dancing; Mother had talked about planning a trip on a boat. In my mind, the boat was the size of the *Queen Elizabeth* and I was the pet passenger. Wendy, by this time, was having piano lessons. So I told her I was going to dance on this boat. She told her mother, so my mother found out. She said I was a liar and made her look silly. We didn't go on a boat for years. Perhaps the boat was my mother's fantasy. After all, the only holidays we ever had were at Grandma's, apart from one holiday in Devon where I let her down dreadfully.

Mother had arranged for us all to go to her old school friend's in Devon. Lena and I were to have a bedroom in the thatched cottage where the friend lived. Mother, Father and Buster were to sleep in the tiny four-berth caravan in the garden.

I refused to sleep in the cottage because I was afraid there might be a thunderstorm and I knew thatched cottages were dangerous. So all five of us crowded into the tiny caravan. Mother's friend was annoyed, Mother felt humiliated, all the more so because she hadn't realized how the friend's social and financial status had risen.

Any difficulties we had with other children, or the neighbours, or anybody else, were always put down by Mother to the fact that they were 'common', or not Catholic. It was this philosophy that got Lena and me expelled from school.

It was an ordinary evening and a group of us were dawdling our way home from school. Wendy was part of the group. A slight difference of opinion occurred between two of the group, nothing serious, just a verbal altercation. Being virtuous I wanted to defend the boy I thought was right. I had a skipping-rope in my hand. I lashed out at his opponent.

I had been too anxious for approval, for I lashed harder than I had meant to, and the rope caught the boy round the face. Big weals swelled up on his cheeks. He complained.

'Serves you right,' I said, uneasily.

'Look what you've done!'

'Let's take him home.'

'I'm telling his mother.'

I stood looking sheepish. 'Well,' I said, 'you shouldn't have called me names.'

'He didn't.'

'Yes, he did,' I said, already believing it. The group had split into two – me, Lena and Wendy, and the rest.

We made our way home. The incident was not discussed but I could not forget it.

The next day the boy was not at school. The headmaster called me aside and asked me about the incident.

'Well,' I said hanging my head. 'He called me a dirty Roman Catholic.'

The headmaster sat back.

'I shall write to your mother,' he said.

I was not at all concerned. If there was one thing guaranteed to inflame mother's paranoia it was a slur against the faith.

Mother was called to the school. True, we had had insults about our religion in our early days at the school but nothing momentous. However, the headmaster decided that if our mother was complaining she should be the one to do something about it.

'I suggest, Mrs Mulligan,' he said, 'that if the girls are not happy here, you remove them and send them to a Roman Catholic school. Then there will be no more problems.'

We weren't exactly expelled, but when Mother recounted the story in later years, that was the word she used. 'Daffodil is a problem. She got herself expelled from school at nine years old.'

'I can't imagine,' Mother used to say, 'what you'll be like when you are grown up.'

The period of growing up, adolescence, was marked by events called 'rows'. I was always led to believe I was the instigator, despite my mother's additional years and wisdom and power.

These rows had a consistent theme: I had done something, or, more often, not done something I had been expected to do, even if I had not been told and did not know it was expected of me. Usually it was expected that I did it and not Lena. It could have been washing up after a meal, about which there were innumerable conflicts. I would wash up and make a fuss about it, Mother would complain that I hadn't done it properly, I would complain that she always complained and that even when I did what she wanted she didn't know how to say thank you properly. My prodigious insight at around eleven or twelve must have unnerved her.

One day there was the row to end all rows. And it did.

'Daffodil, run upstairs and fetch my handbag for me, will you?'

I was reading and resented this intrusion. I ignored her.

'Daffodil, run upstairs and fetch my handbag for me!'

I put the book on my lap and whined impatiently, 'Do I have to?'

'Yes, you do.'

'Run upstairs and fetch your own handbag.'

'What did you say?'

'I said, run upstairs and fetch your own handbag. You always say I never do anything to help you but two or three times a day you ask me to run upstairs and fetch your handbag, and you don't even say thank you when I do.'

'Don't speak to me like that!' said Mother, bristling at the truth.

'I have spoken to you like that. I'm fed up with you always complaining and never saying thank you. You always say how bad I am, never what I do that's good.'

The book was snatched from me and flung across the room.

'You've always got your nose in a book. It't not healthy. Fetch my handbag for me.'

'No.'

The response to that was a slap round the face. Tears spilled down the side of my nose.

'Wendy's mother never hits her.'

'Wendy's mother doesn't have problems with Wendy like I do with you. There's something wrong with you. You're a naughty little girl.'

'No, I'm not,' I cried, unconvinced. 'You're always telling me how bad I am. One day I'll do something really bad, then you'll know that in comparison I'm really good now.'

She shook me by the shoulders.

'You're a wicked girl. If you ever bring an illegitimate baby home on this doorstep, out you go.'

I stopped crying and stared at her, not knowing whether to dwell on the nature of the revelation or the peculiar logic of her statement. How could I go out if I was not in?

I jumped up and stood facing her. 'You're horrid. It would serve you right if I ran away.'

'Where would you go? Auntie Rose? Do you think she'd have you, the way you behave? Don't think I haven't told her.'

My one hope gone, I rushed out of the room, up the stairs and into my bedroom. She followed, wielding a wooden spoon. I banged the door shut. She pushed and shoved and shouted. I let the door go suddenly and she fell in.

I fell on my bed face down, crying loudly, as I usually did on these occasions. Later, when it was dark, I used to pack my attaché case with all my secret documents – diaries, letters, cuttings of favourite film stars – and sit on the back steps pretending to have run away and waiting to hear sounds of concern from the house. They never came and I was forced to creep indoors and into bed, to wake up the next morning subdued but obedient.

Mother started hitting me with the wooden spoon, not unbearably hard but I screamed. It was my last weapon and the windows were open. Suddenly a voice floated up and stopped Mother's antics.

'Are you all right, Daffodil?' It was Wendy's mother.

Mother went to the window and leaned out, panting.

'It's all right, Mrs Robinson,' she gasped, 'Daffodil has been naughty – again – and I'm just giving her a good hiding.'

If I could have smirked through my tears I would have done, but for the fact that she had now also spoiled my reputation in the neighbourhood. Mother was completely at a loss for a moment.

'Get your coat on,' she said suddenly.

'What for?'

'Get your coat on. I'm taking you up to the education office. I'm going to have you put away.'

I knew I was meant to grovel and beg to be allowed to stay at home. I was not beaten yet. Although I felt ashamed, I knew I was not a desperate case. I was well behaved at school. Lena and Buster were instructed to get their coats on too and we were marched up the lane, Mother breathing angrily and loudly through flared nostrils.

At the gates of the education office, Mother stopped.

'I'm prepared to give you a last chance, Daffodil,' she said nobly.

I shrugged. 'I don't want a last chance. You put me in a home. I shan't mind. I shall get away from you and anyway when they've had me for a while they'll find out how nice I am and they'll know there's something wrong with you.'

For a brief moment, I think my head was in danger of being beaten to a pulp against the gates of the education office. Then I knew I had won. I did not at the time realize how big was the victory. I had in fact won the war, not just that battle. She turned towards home. 'I can't do it. Anyway,' she said 'Lena and Buster would miss you. So would I. And I've got the stomach-ache.'

Then we had to run home for Mother to reach the bathroom in time. And I had a lot to ponder upon.

CHAPTER 3

As a result of this confrontation with my mother, I began having long conversations with Wendy. This is not to say that Wendy and I had not had long conversations previously. We had. But now the content became more serious, more personal, more interior. I had read, too, in the agony columns of women's magazines which I perused avidly in search of enlightenment for my particular, unnamed and indefinable problems, that talking about problems helped. Having no notion what my problem was, adolescence brought about the realization that I should do something about it.

I told Wendy about the row. Because it was a wet day we had to stay indoors and because we wanted to talk privately, we went upstairs to her bedroom. Somehow or other I had been relieved of the responsibility of Lena, who was usually expected to accompany me everywhere. This was called 'sharing your friends, Daffodil', because among other things I was reputed to be selfish and unwilling to share with my sister. I was unable to see this myself but was occasionally bothered that I was seen in this way at home. After all, I did not have much experience of Lena sharing with me, expecially her friends, of whom she had none.

Wendy had a beautiful bedroom. It was like something out

of a film, all pink curtains and covers and carpet, frilly lace at the window, a bookcase and a dressing-table with frothy curtains round it. Lena and I shared a room with iron bedsteads, not matching and painted green, green lino with one rug that skidded under Lena's bed if I stepped out of my bed on to it, and under my bed if Lena stepped out of her bed on to it. We had boxes for what were still described as 'toys', despite my attempts to refer to my 'things'. The bedspreads mother had made were nice, but they did not match.

This was the first time I had been in Wendy's bedroom.

'Aren't you lucky!' I said, sinking gently on to the edge of the bed while I admired all the beauty and luxury around me. I had the same feeling as I had when I realized that Wendy's house had a bathroom and ours did not, and that I mustn't talk about it. Why were the Mulligans so different all the time? And why didn't I even fit in with the Mulligans?

Worse was to come. Wendy, it seemed, did not have dreadful rows at home. Wendy expressed the opinion, together with a limited sympathy for me, that my mother was a bit odd. It did not occur to me at the time that Wendy had overheard her mother's opinion of mine. I was at the age when other people's opinions mattered and my contemporary's expressed opinions mattered most. Again I was different. Now it was an odd mother that made me different

'Let's talk about other things,' Wendy said. 'Have you started yet?'

'No,' I said and giggled a bit. 'Have you?'

'Yes,' said Wendy, 'last night. It was terrible. I thought that I was going to die. You wait till you start.'

'But,' I said, 'you're all right now!'

Wendy looked surprised.

'You're lying,' I said. 'It lasts four days, not one evening. And it doesn't hurt.'

Wendy relaxed. 'No. I was only joking. I thought you might have started and I didn't want to be left out.'

'But I would tell you!' I protested.

'Ye-es. But Lena's always around. You can't talk about it, when Lena's around.'

'Well, she's not around today.'

'No. So you can tell me how you're so sure it lasts four days.'

'I read it in my mother's book.'

'Has your mother got a book?' Wendy, usually so tall and aloof, bent forward eagerly. Then she straightened. 'In my mother's book it says . . .'

I knew her mother did not have a book.

'I can get my mother's book,' I boasted. 'She keeps it in the linen chest by her bed. I was in her room last week. She was doing my hair. She picked up the book and pointed to a bit about periods and said "Here – read this!" When I'd read it she took it off me, put it in the linen chest and started talking about holidays.'

'She was embarrassed,' Wendy said with an air of wisdom.

'Yes,' I said, delighted to have discovered another of my mother's weaknesses. 'Does your mother get embarrassed by these things?'

'No,' said Wendy loyally, then covering her own hunger for information. 'But then, she doesn't talk about them.'

I remembered that Wendy had been away from school on the morning we had had sex education, such that it was. I had had to pass on the information, in snippets, when Lena was not around. I realized that of the two of us I was the expert. I could be even more of an expert if I could take a good look at that book of my mother's in the linen chest in her bedroom. I planned that next time Mother went out without me, I would sneak up to her bedroom and read some of it.

Of course, Mother rarely went out and left me at home. Usually it was I who went to the shops if she needed anything. It was ten days or so before she decided to carry out her own errands. I immediately suspected she wanted sanitary towels, otherwise she would have asked me to do her shopping. It was only at the last moment that I realized that I was now old enough to be trusted to look after Lena.

Rigid with chagrin, I watched Mother walk down the road with Buster. Once out of sight, I turned on Lena and started shouting at her.

'I'm not looking after you! You ruin my life. You're a nuisance. Why can't you find your own friends? Why do I always have to tag you around with me? I only want a bit of peace!'

Lena started to cry, protesting that it was not her fault, I should not shout at her and she'd tell Mother.

I called her a tell-tale, slapped her then threatened unmentionable consequences if she stirred from the spot where she was. I then told her I had the stomach-ache and was going to the toilet, and, while she was distracted, I crept upstairs to our parents' bedroom.

Concentrating on reading the book was a problem because I had to perch on the end of the bed in order to keep watch out of the window for Mother's return.

Chapter one was all about conception (after fertilization) and the growth of the baby in the mother's womb. I was fascinated by the diagrams, especially of the birth – there was this plump, placid baby with closed eyes being forced into the world, to face God knows what kind of life, perhaps a mother like mine? It made me feel sad. The next chapters were all about caring for babies and children, their feeding, potty training, development. That was quite interesting. I realized that this was quite an old book and its methods had been tried on me. Then came the chapter on adolescence. I was just reading how girls should be told the facts of life before they start menstruating, and how allowances should be made for adolescent girls' mood changes when I spied two familiar silhouettes moving down the road. Reluctantly, I closed the book, lifted the lid of the linen chest, put the book exactly where I had found it, smoothed the bedspread and crept downstairs just in time to catch Lena sneaking biscuits from the kitchen cupboard. By the time Mother came in I was making such a fuss about Lena's misdemeanours that she and I both forgot about my own.

During the weeks and months that followed I made several secret trips to the linen chest. I became quite well informed about adolescence, marriage (the Big Question), sexual intercourse, which I had a simple idea about, but which sounded absolutely revolting. The afternoon I read that section I vowed to become a school teacher and never marry. After that was contraception, which was an added disgust to sexual intercourse. I was relieved to read that Roman Catholics were not allowed to use contraceptives. Then there was masturbation, homosexuality, impotence and frigidity. Sometimes I had to wait for days to convey this information to Wendy often in an unsucessful code. In fact, my coded information on contraception, which made it sound not only revolting but totally impossible, led me into some very serious trouble.

It was a wet Saturday evening. Lena and I had been down to the church to confession. On the way out I stopped in the porch to survey the Catholic Truth Society pamphlets with the aim of furthering my research. I had confirmed that, for Catholics, contraception was definitely not allowed, neither was masturbation. Homosexuality was forbidden also, at least, homosexual acts were, but neither the pamphlet nor Mother's book gave enlightenment on what they were. I scanned the pamphlets and decided that a lot of things seemed to be wrong according to the church and began to question whether I should be reading Mother's book at all.

When we arrived home we found that we had visitors, some friends of my mother's. Daddy did not have friends. I assumed he shared Mother's and she did not mind. I soon realized that they had a bottle of wine – a rare occasion – and that Lena and I were tiresome distractions. On the spur of the moment I decided on a plan.

Upstairs I went. I fetched my school satchel from my bedroom, crept into Mother and Daddy's room, lifted the book from the linen chest, crept downstairs, out of the back door and round to Wendy's. Her family were watching television. I could have joined them, as Lena and I did occasionally, but I beckoned to Wendy and we crept upstairs to her bedroom.

We had a lovely evening. Wendy was totally engrossed in the book. I watched her read it, making comments every so often.

'See, I told you.'

'Yes, but you didn't *explain.*'

'Well, the book doesn't explain,' I said. 'It doesn't say how long it takes.'

'It doesn't say a lot.' Wendy said.

'Oh, if you don't like it . . .'

'Oh, it's not that. I expect you can't put these things into words. Romance is about *feelings*, Daffie, not words.'

'Romance?' I said.

'That's what it's about,' Wendy said, wisely.

'It doesn't sound romantic to me,' I protested. 'It sounds – disgusting. I think I'll be a nun.' In the light of all the information I had gathered, this seemed the best course of action.

'Is *that* why Catholics become nuns?' Wendy asked, as if light had dawned.

'Oh, no,' I said hurriedly, realizing that with one sentence I had just undone months of PR for the church. 'Catholics believe that sex is beautiful,' I added quoting a CTS pamphlet.

'There you are. If it's beautiful, it's romantic,' Wendy said.

I began to feel a little uneasy. Wendy, until I educated her, had been almost totally ignorant about sex but now she was captivated by the idea of it while I found the notion of it very unappealing.

By the time I left, we both felt we knew a lot more and what the book had not told us we had conjectured. I returned home, the book in my satchel, feeling less mystified.

I had a shock when I realized that Mother was in her bedroom, so I went upstairs and put my, fastened, satchel in its usual place by my bed. I waited all Sunday for a safe opportunity to return the book to the linen chest. By Monday morning, none had arisen, so I found myself taking it to school.

During Monday afternoon, we had a boring science lesson, more boring than usual. Wendy and I sat at the back. We were allowed to because we were considered quite well behaved in lessons. In fact, we had little to do with other pupils and kept ourselves to ourselves.

The science teacher droned on about atoms and molecules and I was thinking about sperm and ova and sexual intercourse. I wondered how often people did it. Did the book say? I pulled it out of my satchel and, under the cover of the laboratory benches, flipped over the pages. Wendy's eyes bulged, then gleamed.

So engrossed were we that we did not hear the teacher call our names. We did not hear the footsteps marching towards us, nor sense the atmosphere of expectancy as the rest of the class watched us.

'Daffodil Mulligan.' roared the teacher. 'What is it that takes up your attention more than my lesson?

Mother's book was snatched from my lap.

'What is this? *Sex in Marriage*.' The class roared with laughter. The teacher blushed and was silenced. 'I will see you both at the end of the lesson.'

We were seen at the end of the lesson.

'What, Daffodil Mulligan, do you mean by bringing a

book of this nature to school?'

I hung my head. Oh God, was I in trouble now!

'I don't know.'

'Come with me, both of you, to the Head.'

The Head was less embarrassed than the science teacher. Wendy was given a detention. A letter was going home to my parents so that the book could be returned to its rightful owner, then my punishment would be decided, together with my parents.

I spent a sleepless night. I planned an asthma attack for the morning so that I could be at home when the postman arrived and intercept the letter. But Lena intervened, with a bad stomach-ache and I swear if I'd had the worst asthma attack of my life, it would have paled in comparison to Lena's belly-ache.

When I came home that evening, Lena was better and nothing was said to me. But the next night it was. The letter arrived on Wednesday morning and Mother was waiting for me when I reached home. She was beside herself with fury. Only years later did I understand her mortification, but then I had not realized that the book fell open and the spine was broken at the section on frigidity.

Mother screamed, screeched and shouted at me. She threatened me, she made promises, she told me how bad I was, what a dirty mind I had, that I was a thief and that she was ashamed of me. I threatened to scream if she hit me. But, apart from that, I said very little. I was dreading the interview with the Head the next day and it was that which eventually made me cry.

Mother appeared to soften a little. To protect me, so that my father would not know what a dreadful girl I was, she would not tell him about it unless the Head had anything else bad to say about me. I was not so slow as she thought and realized that she was too embarrassed to tell my father.

Mother took to her bed that evening with a bad back, and

Daddy and I cooked tea and put Buster to bed. Whether Mother was avoiding my father because she had something to hide from him or whether she was genuinely unwell, her condition worsened by my behaviour, I am unable to say. What I do know is that my feelings that evening were of relief that I was not being threatened by mother's taunting glances, and of alarmed guilt that I had made her ill.

The next morning, Mother struggled to the school to keep her appointment with the Head at eleven o'clock, some two hours after I had struggled, on very shaky legs, to get to school at the usual time.

The Head was surprisingly pleasant, to me and to Mother. I was told that I should not bring such literature to school, that if I or my friends had any questions about sex, we were to speak to our mothers, or our teachers, and would I please make sure other girls were told that, if I was questioned about the incident. I was advised to concentrate on my school work and not read books of *any* description under the desks or benches during lessons. My punishment was to be detained after school for half an hour for the next two evenings.

I thought this was fair and agreed with the Head when my agreement was sought. Mother, however, had different ideas. She sat shifting uncomfortably on her chair either from pain or embarrassment, which increased when the book was handed back to her.

'I think,' she began, 'that you are letting my daughter off lightly. She is beginning to be quite a problem at home. I am getting very worried about her. After all, I did not give her this book. She stole it from me. It's an old book, not worth anything. Very old-fashioned,' said my enlightened mother, 'but she stole it and we have never known Daffodil to steal anything before.'

If I had not been so shocked I would have, for the first time in my life, called her a bitch. She's split on me, I thought. My eyes filled with tears, my cheeks burned. Instead of panicking, I tried calmly to think why she was doing this. Understanding came quickly. She was normally ashamed to admit outside home that she found me a problem but recently I had robbed her of her ultimate weapon, the 'good hiding'. She was now appealing to superior powers.

'Mrs Mulligan,' said the Head. 'how your daughter behaves at home is really not in my sphere of influence. That is your problem and how you deal with it is up to you and your husband. All I know is, this was an isolated incident and Daffodil, although she could work harder, has been no problem to us.'

Mother took a deep breath, straightened her back and said: 'No, we are getting it all at home. Her father and I are very worried.'

'How can Daddy be worried,' I burst out, 'if he doesn't even know about this?'

There was a silence. Mother's cheeks burned now. The Head looked embarrassed and began nodding, with a wise air, not looking at either of us.

'I'm afraid I shall have to leave you in a moment, Mrs Mulligan.' said the Head, 'I have a sixth-form lesson. Unless you have anything to say to Daffodil, I suggest she rejoins her class.'

Tight-lipped, mother said 'No', and rose stiffly.

I returned to my class feeling not smug, or righteous, or victorious, nor cowed or guilty or worried. But just nice and ordinary. I was not bad at school, nor very good. At home I now felt I was not as bad as I had thought and probably in some ways even good. I was ordinary.

Back in the classroom, I ignored the questioning, perhaps admiring, glances from the others and settled down to enjoy a moderately good geography lesson from a moderately good geography teacher. The rest of the day, even the detention, was quite ordinary. And Daddy and I had to cook the tea and see Buster to bed again that evening.

CHAPTER 4

Time went on. Mother's health deteriorated and damands on me to help out at home increased. The book vanished from the linen chest and I caught a glimpse of it in the dustbin one morning. I was not very concerned for I knew a lot of it by heart anyway. And besides, I had now discovered the public library. There were books there that I did not have the courage to take out, but Wendy and I spent many a spare half hour hidden between the shelves, reading with bright eyes, pink cheeks and a furtive air.

'Gosh,' I would say, 'have you read this?'

'No,' Wendy would whisper back, 'have a look at this, though. Do people *really* do that?'

Wendy was interested in practice – she wanted to do it as soon as possible. I was more interested in theory – my research was to discover whether it was worth doing.

That summer, as usual, Auntie Rose, Uncle Wack and Cousin Ritchie paid us a short visit. This one was like all previous visits and followed some sort of prescribed ritual. Mother suddenly felt slightly better and did a little more housework, with which I helped. Lena and I were ordered to tidy our bedrooms, and I found myself running hither and thither on errands. A large joint was bought for Sunday dinner and the whole of Sunday morning was spent sacrificially burning it. Mother always claimed to be an expert cook, but the proof of the pudding was in the left-overs. She had never mastered the electric oven, nor cleaned it either, I think. Consequently, at Christmas and other festivities the kitchen filled with a smokey haze, eyes smarted and windows were opened wide. Years later, Auntie Rose told me that Mother's Sunday dinners were a perennial joke and she and Uncle Wack always delayed arrival at our house in the hope that we would have had our meal without waiting for them.

On this, as on other occasions, we children mooned around for hours, watching the clock, chewing bread and jam because we were hungry. The joint burned, the roast potatoes were black on the outside and Mother hovered by the window muttering, 'They must have got held up. I hope they haven't had an accident.'

The car drew up outside some two hours past the estimated time of arrival. Mother complained, Auntie Rose was defensive, Uncle Wack puffed on his pipe we all got hugged and kissed and Daddy stayed in the background.

Then, when Mother started serving the meal, her back suddenly got worse, she carried on bravely and Auntie Rose was made to feel like a worm for having mentioned that they had had 'a bite on the way'. We all sat down to the meal, using Mother's best china, linen, cutlery and glass and inevitably Lena spilt gravy on the tablecloth, Ritchie broke a glass and complained that the Yorkshire pudding was tough.

After all this, and the washing-up, the grown-ups sat around exchanging news and gossip. We children hovered and we bribed with sweets and chocolate by Auntie Rose to go away and amuse ourselves. I had no problem with this. There was a ritual game that Auntie Rose and Uncle Wack played with me. I knew that whenever they visited us while Grandma was staying with Auntie June, they would take me, and usually Lena as well, back with them for a holiday. Most years it was the only holiday we had. However, I was not expected to take this understanding for granted so had to play the waiting game until an hour before they left and either Auntie Rose or Uncle Wack would say, 'Well, girls, what are your plans? Do you have time to come and spend a few days with us?' A few days meant as long as we wanted and in the summer could be more than a month.

We had to pretend to be surprised and say 'Oh, yes, could we really? That would be lovely.' This last minute cliff-hanging suspense was no good to me. I needed at least a week to pack my case, not only with clothes, but my diaries, documents, pens, reading matter, list of people for whom to buy presents and to send postcards. Under my bed was my case, already packed, but just waiting for last-minute additions.

On this occasion I went up to my room and took the case from under my bed. I checked the contents against the list stuck on the inside of the lid, dithered over an additional T-shirt, or should I add tights instead of socks? Really, this was more an exercise in anticipation than organization. The door behind me was pushed open quietly. I jumped guiltily. Auntie Rose came in. She was quite different from Mother although they were sisters. She was plumper and rounder, had auburn hair, a girlish manner and laughed a lot.

'Oooh! Daffie, what've you got there? Going somewhere, are you?'

'Well,' I said confused. 'I just thought . . .'

'Oh, what a pity. We were going to ask you if you'd like to come back with us. But if you've got other plans . . .'

'I haven't. I haven't. Honest. Can we come back with you? Please?'

Auntie Rose sat on the bed. 'What've you been doing to upset your mum?'

'What do you mean?' Terror gripped me. Auntie Rose doesn't want me there any more.

'Your mum says you've been misbehaving.'

'Did she tell you . . . about . . . the . . . book?' I asked nervously.

'What book?'

'What did she say?'

'Just that you had been naughty and she couldn't control you any more and she was worried about the effect you might have on Lena.'

Oh, was she! I thought. 'What did Daddy say? I asked.

'He wasn't there. Anyway, I said I thought it was probably your age, or her age and anyway you could do with a rest from her and why doesn't Lena help more. So I said we'd take you back with us and not Lena. Lena's never so keen to come, is she?'

I grinned. 'Did you really say all that? Thanks. Yes, I'd love to come. But what about me being difficult? Are you sure?'

'Oh,' Auntie Rose stood and waved her hands impatiently. 'Don't you take too much notice of Lady Mulligan. I don't'

'Why do you call her Lady Mulligan?'

'Oh, she's got airs and graces and she's nobody really. Don't you tell her I said so, though, will you?'

'No . . . No. Sometimes . . . sometimes I hate her.' I ventured. I had not even dared to be so extreme even in my confidences to Wendy.

'Oh, so do I!' said Auntie Rose, dismissing my burden in her mind and mine. 'She started off on the wrong foot with you, giving you that silly name.'

I was very sensitive about my name. 'I think it's silly. But I had hoped no one else did.'

'Do you know how you got the name? She worked for some aristocrat before she was married, someone named Delphine del Monte. *She* thought – and so did I, because I believed her – that the name was Daffodil Monty. She'd never seen it written down, you see.'

My response was a mixture of anger and amusement. I laughed loudly, very loudly, so that my mother downstairs would hear and wonder if I was laughing at her.

Auntie Rise caught hold of my hand. 'Come on down to tea. I've brought some fruit cake and angel cake. I think your mum's made some rock cakes again. And Ritchie's been dipping his fingers in the triffle. See the funny side!'

I stayed with Auntie Rose, Uncle Wack and Ritchie for four weeks that summer. A great fuss was made of me as the daughter they had never had. I also wondered if I was the daughter my parents did not want. It would have been fairer if Auntie Rose had had me and Mother hadn't – and nicer. Auntie Rose asked her friend round to cut and style my hair. I was taken on shopping expeditions and bought things – not a lot, just one or two items like a petticoat, a scarf, a bracelet. Uncle Wack drove into the mountains one Sunday and at the roadside, among heather and bracken, sheep droppings and litter bins, picnic chairs and tables, a primus stove, a huge hamper of luxury foods like bought cakes, tinned salmon and cold omelettes were brought out of the boot of the car. I played in the street, stayed up late, watched television and wore make-up. I even had a row with Auntie Rose. What it was about I can't remember, but I do recall threatening to go home. I pounded upstairs, squashed everything into my case and dashed dramatically from the house and marched in the direction of the bus station. What I would have done when I reached it, I don't know, but Auntie Rose did not allow it to happen. Unlike Mother, who could sit out a ten-day siege in cold silence, Auntie Rose, very upset, rushed after me. I didn't want to go home, Auntie Rose didn't want me to go home and she showed it. When I glanced over my shoulder and saw her, I felt so relieved. I stopped and let her catch up with me. She took the case from me.

'Come here, you silly girl,' she said. 'You don't want to be here at this time of night. It was here I saw a man expose himself a couple of months ago.'

'Where?' I demanded, looking round wide-eyed, and we both laughed.

I had to go home eventually because school was starting again. It was raining when Mother, Lena and Buster met me off the coach. Lena was hanging on to Mother's arm looking smug. I didn't look at her after the first glance because I knew she was trying to tell me she had had a better time at home that I had at Auntie Rose's.

That evening I went round to Wendy's to tell her about my holiday.

Wendy had had a good holiday too.

'Guess what!' she said, shutting her bedroom door and lowering her voice to a whisper.

'Has something happened?'

'Yes.' She paused, all pink and more animated than I had ever seen her. I knew instinctively that her news was something to do with sex. Had she done it? I wondered frantically, both fearsome and envious.

'I've got a boyfriend.' she announced.

I tried not to let my nasty feelings show.

'Have you really?' I managed.

'Yes,' Wendy was not interested in my finer reactions. She just wanted to talk. 'I've been dying to tell you. I met him on holiday. He lives here, but the other side of the town. He's in the sixth form at the boys' school over there. His name is Roderick.'

'Ooh!' I said. 'Have you kissed him?'

'Ye-e-e-ss!'

'Was it . . . nice?'

'Ye-e-e-ss!'

'How did you know how to kiss?' This was the sort of thing that bothered me.

'I just did what he did.'

'Does your mother know?'

'That I kissed him?'

'No, silly. About him?'

'Yes. She met his parents when we were in Poole.'

I fell silent. All the good that four weeks with Auntie Rose had done was cancelled out in ten minutes with Wendy. I was angry, envious, afraid and worried. What had Wendy got that I hadn't got? Why had I not met a boyfriend while I was on holiday? All the freedom that Auntie Rose gave me would have surely given me the opportunity.

Then I knew. There was something wrong with me. Mother was right. I was a dreadful girl and, furthermore, it showed. No boy would look at me because it showed.

I was in despair and turned to the public library in the next few days, for comfort – alone.

I gathered enough courage to mention Wendy's boyfriend to Mother.

'Wendy,' I stated, 'has a boyfriend.'

'Yes, so her mother tells me,' said Mother. 'Forward little hussey. I wonder Mrs Robinson allows it. I know where Wendy will end up. She'll get herself in the family way, that's what'll happen to her. Before she's eighteen she'll find herself pushing a pram up and down these hills. You mark my words.'

I felt Mother was wishing this destiny on Wendy.

'She *is* fifteen,' I said.

'Fifteen, fifteen?' I flinched at the way Mother shrieked. 'You are nearly fifteen. If I thought you were carrying on like that, I'd tan your backside. I'm not having you coming home here with a baby. If you get yourself into trouble, my girl, out you go.'

There was not much I could say in answer to all this, but I wondered to myself at the strength of Mother's feelings on the subject.

She took my silence as indicative of sympathy with Wendy

– which it wasn't. I hated her for the turmoil she was causing me.

'I hope you haven't been carrying on with boys while you've been at Auntie Rose's?'

'No!' I said, aghast. *Boys!* Did she really imagine I could attract them in the plural? Could she not see I couldn't get the interest of even one, puny, weedy little specimen?

I was now in the fifth form at school. The end was in sight. I assessed all the boys in my form and decided it was hopeless; they were either devastatingly handsome, in which case there was a group of fluttering girls around them all the time and I refused to compete (as if the question of doing so ever arose), or they were wet or ugly, often both. Eventually I settled for a boy called Brian Jones, whom I claimed to worship from afar and that at least saved my pride. Also, Brian Jones was tall, had a very deep voice, five o'clock shadow and a square jaw. At least I was aiming at men, not boys. Brian Jones was painfully shy and would have died of shame at the thought of Daffodil Mulligan of the fat legs and sex book being interested in him. So as neither of us was likely to speak to the other, it was a very silent, passive affair.

The fifth year at school was quite fun apart from the work. Our teachers arranged educational visits for us, to help us with our examinations. We went to see *Macbeth* at Stratford-upon-Avon. I had never been to the theatre before and was captivated. Wendy had seen pantomimes and lesser works, but I, nothing. Other pupils, whose fathers were such god-like creatures as teachers, solicitors, bank clerks, librarians and clergymen had been to the West End to see productions, some of them more than once. My entrancement was a source of amusement to those near me.

We were taken to the opera, to see *La Traviata*. I cried. They laughed. But I loved it. We were taken to an orchestral concert at the Royal Festival Hall and shown round the

National Gallery. I was amazed to see so many paintings of sacred scenes with naked women in them, and worse, naked men. There were willies everywhere. Shock interfered with artistic appraisal. I commented tentatively to Wendy but she did not seem to be reeling as I was. I felt uneasy. Was Wendy's reaction due to the fact that she was not a Catholic, or was it because she had seen 'one of those' in Real Life? The thought made me panic. If the latter were true, what was I doing consorting with a fallen woman, a contaminated person, someone who was no longer innocent? I wanted to ask Wendy, but apart from my reluctance to ask such a personal question, there was my fear of her answer.

I knew exactly how she would be: 'Oh yes, Daffodil,' she would say airily, 'Yes, I've seen one. But when you've seen one you've seen them all!' That was what Auntie Rose had said when I questioned her about the flasher: 'When you've seen one, you've seen them all.' But I didn't want to see one, not really. Some things in life are sacred.

Many of these educational visits entailed journeys to or through London. Although I had lived within a day trip of the capital all my life, I had paid very few and only necessary visits to it and knew little about it except what Mother had conveyed. Mother had always spoken darkly of London. From her I understood that London was a pit of dirt, violence and sex. No decent girl ever thought of visiting London much less of living there. Everyone in London was poor, criminal and common. As a countrywoman, Mother feared the big city and everything it stood for.

So my visits to London were even more educational than their intent. What I saw was a city of unexpected beauty; there were parks, trees, rivers, lakes, gardens, wide streets, elegant buildings – and the sun shone. Also, the people whom I saw through the windows of the coaches I was in, looked absolutely ordinary.

One day, Wendy and I planned a trip of our own to

London. We wanted to explore the Houses of Parliament, Westminster Abbey, Trafalgar Square on our own. We took some books out of the library, plotted our route on maps and then asked permission to go.

Wendy's mother did not hesitate. My mother hesitated a lot. So we asked Wendy's mother to have a word with her. Reluctantly, and issuing dire warnings, Mother agreed. Daddy pointed out that fifteen and sixteen-year-olds lived in London. Mother retorted that she did not have a high opinion of how they lived.

'Don't get talking to strangers,' Mother said. 'Keep out of pubs. Don't drink, or smoke. Don't get buying any pills or sweets from people and don't let anyone stick needles into you. Don't sit on the seats in public lavatories and keep where there are plenty of people – but not too many.'

If Mother had continued I think I might have lost my nerve . . .

The trip was a success. I began to become quite excited by all this dipping into life and culture. Realization dawned that this was what education was. My confidence began to grow again for the first time since Wendy and Roderick.

I came home from school one evening after a talk with one of my teachers. 'I've decided what I want to do,' I announced at tea time.

Mother and Daddy looked at each other in relief. Another problem with me lately had been my inability to decide the direction of my life. My parents wanted me to be a nurse when I was older. But what I was expected to do until then neither I nor they knew.

'I want to go to university and study English and French. I want to stay on to the sixth form.'

The silence that followed surprised me. I had expected my intentions to be received joyously. I looked up.

'You can't,' said Mother.

'Yes, I can. I've been talking to my teacher. If I . . .'

'You can't. You've got to leave school and get a job. We can't afford to keep you in the sixth form. We can't afford to send you to university.'

'You can get a grant,' I said.

'No, we can't!' thundered my usually mild father. 'You're leaving school and going to be a nurse. We haven't got the money for your fancy ideas. And your mother's health – think about that!'

He left the room to calm down, taking Lena and Buster with him. Once again an issue was reduced to confrontation between Mother and me, although I didn't see it like that at the time. I just thought it was me being selfish and greedy and expecting more from life than I was entitled to. I accused Mother and Daddy of being afraid of me being better than they were, and I told Mother how bitterly I resented her ill-health being brought into the question of my future and I knew why she was ill, I knew it was only a way of avoiding sex.

Mother threw a plate of bread and butter at me, observed with unexpected calm that if that was how my mind worked, the sooner I started nursing and dealt with my preoccupation with bodies, the better. She then returned to bed and stayed there for a week.

I left school that summer with two 'O'-levels and an on-going curiosity about sex.

CHAPTER 5

On leaving school I was found a dreadful job in a dreadful office with dreadful people. After three months I left and worked in a shop selling babys' and children's clothes. When I had the opportunity of what sounded like a promising job in another office, I left the shop, only to find myself out of the frying pan into the fire. I longed to return to shop work, where at least the faces before you changed. I found a job in a ladies' dress shop, but while I was still on probation there, I heard of another, better paid job in a dry-cleaner's down the road and took the morning off for an interview. The manager of the dress shop sacked me. Fortunately I had been offered the job in the dry-cleaner's. All this happened within twelve months of leaving school and I still did not have what I considered to be a proper boyfriend.

I stayed at the dry-cleaner's for a whole year, not because I liked it but because I was beginning to feel a little ashamed. Mother would not discuss my job with me, nor would she discuss my employment situation with anyone else. Auntie Rose used to write 'What is Daffodil doing now? Is she still at that office?' or 'that shop' Mother would write back and say yes, Daffodil, as far as she knew, was still in the same job. If I had to write to Auntie Rose I felt obliged to be equally evasive in order to protect Mother's sensibilities.

During one of Auntie Rose's and Uncle Wack's visits, I did confess to Auntie Rose the number of jobs that I had had, and even she looked concerned. The old feeling, that had never been totally eradicated anyway, that there was something wrong with Daffodil Mulligan, returned in strength. If Auntie Rose doubted me there must be something wrong.

Around this time I discovered psychology. This was due to Wendy who had landed, a plum little job in the public library. And she stayed there. Wendy's problem was boyfriends. She was unable to keep them. (Not that I considered that to be as insurmountable a problem as mine – not being able to find one.) Roderick had slipped through her fingers soon after *Macbeth* – or was it *La Traviata*? A whole queue seemed to have appeared and Wendy went through them one by one. She offered me her cast-offs sometimes and even tried to make up a foursome, but naturally picked the best one for herself.

Wendy had access to everything in the library, got to know the stock and thought I would be interested in Freud because he wrote about sex.

How right she was. And how interesting was my reading during slack times at the dry-cleaner's. I learned, to my shame, that my suggestion to my mother as to her reason for being ill could have contained an element of truth. Apparently, my fear, avoidance or preoccupation with sex could have been projected on to her. That was an awful thought. I didn't like to think I feared something that the women's magazines claimed unanimously was natural, indeed beautiful. Perhaps there was something wrong with me. But no, according to the psychologists that was adolescent's lament: 'There's something wrong with me. I'm not like the others.'

Then I discovered Penis Envy. I really had difficulty in grasping that one. Could females possibly be envious of something so apparently vulnerable? I certainly could not identify penis envy in myself. In fact, I was extremely glad I did not have one, especially when Auntie Rose informed me that a friend of hers had been to Rome and the Vatican museum was full of ancient statues that had this apparently precious organ broken off! I imagined that hoards of insanely envious Roman women had rampaged through the Eternal City snapping them off like brittle icicles. But perhaps this was why they were always so carefully concealed in real life. On the other hand, it was not women who had painted all those pictures in the National Gallery. Every one had been painted by a man. And so had all the paintings featuring women with naked thighs and huge breasts. Was breast envy the female equivalent of penis envy?

I was instantly converted to Jung.

Funnily enough, the day I began to explore the library's stock of Jungian psychology, I met someone there whom I had not seen for nearly two years – Brian Jones.

I was so surprised but hesitated to draw attention to my presence. He was earnestly thumbling through a volume that looked just as earnest as himself.

'Excuse me,' I said, 'but aren't you Brian Jones? I was in your form at school.' To my ears it sounded like a schoolgirl's introduction. Be light, I told myself, smile. Be ready to ask questions. Men like talking about themselves. That much I had gleaned from the agony columns of women's magazines.

Brian Jones dragged his attention from the book and looked me up and down. 'Yes,' he said. And the one word seemed to imply that as I hadn't troubled to speak to him in the five years we were in the form together, why bother now?

I felt my face go red and turned away. There was a stool behind me, to enable readers to reach the higher shelves, so I stepped up on it to give my attention to psychology before making a too obviously hasty move from that corner. I felt something touch my leg, but attached no importance to it. Then I felt it again, much higher this time, well above my fat knee. I froze, then turned. It was Brian Jones's hand . . .

In my confusion and anxiety to get away I nearly fell off the stool. I hurried out of the library into a light drizzle that cooled my burning cheeks. I was so ashamed. What had Brian Jones seen in my voice and manner that had revealed my desperate interest and curiosity about sex? Did other people notice it, too? Was I giving myself away all the time? Was this some dark and dreadful secret I was trying, unsuccessfully, to hide?

'It wasn't my fault. It wasn't my fault,' I kept muttering to myself all the way home.

Two weeks later Wendy told me she was going out with Brian Jones.

I changed my job again. Mother was tight-lipped about it. I was unsure whether to feel guilty or not until one evening, during an argument concerning my inability to settle in a job, I retorted, 'You should have let me stay on at school,' and instantly I realized I had found a way of punishing my parents. After all the glory she had claimed from the three of us going to the grammar school (for by this time both Lena and Buster were there too) she could now pay the price of not letting me take full advantage of it all by facing the scorn of friends, neighbours and relatives when she had to admit that Daffodil was being a problem about work.

My new job was as a clerk in a big office in a factory. I had scorned such posts before, but was much happier here than I had been anywhere else. There were many girls of my own age, and I began to make friends other than Wendy. They were not the kind of girls my mother approved of, but I was learning rapidly that approval did not make friends. Talk among them was always about boyfriends. Some of them, like Rita and Joan, were engaged to be married and it appeared that with money worries, in-law problems and the finer details of the wedding ceremony (such as, five or six bridesmaids and do I want cousin Anne who is ugly?), tiffs with fiancés were not unknown and Rita and Joan occasionally came to work with red eyes and enlisted sympathy over coffee, lunch times or in the ladies and went off at five thirty with advice and resolve to put matters right.

After about six weeks I found myself permanently in a group of six girls, including Rita and Joan. I had deduced that one of them, Betty, plump and shy, had never had a boyfriend either. The girls had, without any discussion or scheming, taken Betty under their wing and were grooming her. Her diet was carefully watched and if she appeared at the table with any food on her tray that did not meet with their strict – and well-informed – dieting standards, she was sent gently back to the counter to change it for something more acceptable. Sometimes, in the lunch hour, Jenny, who had a reputation for style and fashion in the group, would go with Betty to help her choose clothes. Or Joan would offer to set her hair. When, about eight months after I had joined them, Betty was a stone lighter, with permed curly hair and eye make-up, and rumour had it that Colin, in Export, had more than once inquired about her, excitement ran high. Within a week, Betty had a date.

Once I was well in with the group, they ceased to have qualms about asking very personal questions.

'What's your boyfriend's name?' Rita asked me one lunch time.

'I don't have a boyfriend,' I said with slightly less shame than I would have a few weeks earlier.

'Oh, why's that? A bad experience?' Rita was going to draw me out, I could tell.

'Well, sort of,' I said, thinking of Brian Jones. 'Actually,' I burst out confidingly, for they seemed experts, 'I don't seem to meet the right kind.'

Rita nodded wisely. 'You don't get much chance,' she said, 'with your mother being ill on and off.'

'Yes,' I was so relieved. 'And she wouldn't approve, you know. She's so old-fashioned. And . . . and . . . I've got fat legs.'

'Exercise,' said Rita. 'I've got a book at home. It tells you how to lose weight off your thighs. Yours are quite heavy.'

Rita didn't spare my feelings. And she allowed me no excuses. 'Join things,' she said. 'You don't go out enough. And if you do get a date, your mother needn't know. Just tell her you're going to dancing classes, or whatever.'

'Oh, I couldn't tell her lies,' I lied.

''Course you can. You'll have to, for your own sake. That mother of yours sounds a right old hag.'

Is it possible to feel incredible relief and consuming guilt at the same time?

'What's more,' Rita went on, 'that sister of yourse should help more.'

'Oh, she does a bit,' I said, feeling that I didn't really deserve all this support because I hadn't made it clear that at home I was, always had been and probably always would be, a considerable problem and source of worry. 'Lena's studying for exams. She can't spare too much time.'

'Exams!' In one contemptuous explosion Rita dismissed the education system and all it stood for. 'What you want is a bit of life, love. You take my word for it.'

It was arranged that Betty and I should go to the local dance at the town hall the following Saturday evening. This was, from what they said, the venue for meeting boyfriends, and those whose steadies or fiancés were not acquired at work, had sorted themselves out one at the town hall.

I didn't want to go, but Betty was nervous but eager to have a companion, so I agreed to go. Obedient to Rita, I told Mother I was going to spend the evening at Betty's.

I hated it. So did Betty. We left early, bought fish and chips in the High Street, then strolled down by the river wondering why men didn't seem to like fat legs, it was their loss anyway and we weren't going to bother to chase them, they could chase us.

I took Rita's advice and joined things. I joined the dramatic society. I joined the Caledonian society because I had seen a display by their Scottish country dance team and thought the men looked promising. To be accepted, I said my grandfather was Scottish. He was actually Irish, but that was the nearest I could offer. And I joined the new church youth club. This meant that I suddenly had a very active social life, which gave the lie to my claim about Mother's claim on me, so I just hoped that Lena never met Rita.

At the dramatic society I met my first boyfriend. I thought it was going to be the beginning of the end of my troubles. Instead of that it was just the beginning.

His name was Peter. He walked home with me after my second meeting of the dramatic society. He wanted to be an actor. I was not too impressed by him but thought he was kind to walk me home, even though he lived not far away, and he asked questions about me. I was flattered by his interest in me.

After several weeks of this routine, and after I had described my enthralment when I had made trips to the theatre in London with the school, he suggested that we might go to the theatre in London together one evening. There was a play he rather wanted to see and he was sure I would enjoy it. He suggested that we went to London together the following Saturday to book the tickets.

Only after I had told Mother that a group of us from the dramatic society were going to the theatre did I realize that both the theatre visit and the trip to book the tickets were the nearest things in my life to a date.

Oh, wait till I tell Rita tomorrow morning! Wait till I tell

Wendy tomorrow night! My reputation was saved!

Peter himself did not make much of an impression on me. He was terribly vain, and some of his ways annoyed me, if not embarrassed me. He would talk loudly and exaggeratedly so I knew he was not performing just for me but for everyone around. He was small, my height but thinner than I was. His features were regular but unremarkable. Mostly he talked about himself except when he seemed to feel he had overdone that and he focused on me to redress the balance. He worked in a bank which made him eminently respectable in Mother's eyes on the one occasion she met him.

Rita was extremely pleased with my progress. Wendy, still seeing Brian Jones, was unimpressed. I, however, did not need to impress her. All I wanted was for Wendy to see that I, too, had a boyfriend and being a Mulligan was not, after all, a handicap.

The trip to London to book the tickets was an enjoyable outing. I enjoyed the actual theatre visit too. On the way home from the railway station, Peter asked what should we do next Saturday. My stomach turned over as I realized he was interested in me, and did not merely want company for the theatre. We decided on a day out to London again. He would come to my home to pick me up. This meant I would have to tell Mother I had a boyfriend but I would deal with that later. Meanwhile, Peter had taken my hand. I walked along the road with him feeling very sophisticated, and just wondering if Wendy would, by some chance, be peeping out of the window. If she was, I never found out because of what happened next. Peter kissed me! My first kiss! I even remember the date. For a kiss, it was not remarkable; it was very chaste in fact, and much the same as the good-bye kisses Mother and Daddy gave me. I said goodnight to Peter, let myself indoors and floated upstairs to bed in a lovely glow of normality.

To my surprise, Mother was not at all disapproving.

'Yes, well' she said, 'I think you're old enough easily, by now. And as you don't seem to want a career, the best thing you can do is get married.'

'I didn't say anything about getting married,' I gasped, appalled, and hoping she would not say anything so outrageous to Peter when he knocked on the door on Saturday. 'I'm just going out with him. Once. He's the first boyfriend I've ever had.'

'Yes, well, I hope you're not going to be one of those common girls who floats around from one boy to another. No one will want to marry you if you behave like that.'

Rita was overjoyed, especially about the kiss, although I didn't tell her it was the first time it had happened to me. With the girls at work I maintained an air of mystery and hurt about my recent past with regard to the opposite sex. It was an unspoken rule that painful parts did not have to be revealed. My past was painful because it was an absolute void!

Peter saw me home after the meeting of the dramatic society that week and again he held my hand and kissed me goodnight on the doorstep.

Saturday was a pleasant day. I saw St Paul's, the Tower of London, I walked over Tower Bridge and sat by the river. The journey to and from London was becoming familiar. On the way home, Peter put his arm round my shoulders. Walking from the station, he put his arm around my waist so, after a while, I put my arm around his. I reflected, as we walked up the road thus, that maybe I would be giving up the Caledonian society and the youth club before long.

We reached my front door. I was expecting the usual kiss, after which, my key in my hand, I would venture the carefully rehearsed 'Would you like to come in for a cup of coffee?' as suggested by Rita and all the agony aunts I had ever read.

He did kiss me. I raised my key to the lock, only to find

another kiss bearing down on me, much more passionate this time. His hands were suddenly everywhere, and they finally and quickly settled on the front of my dress, then he undid the button and his hand was inside my dress.

In a panic, I pushed him away, shoved the key in the lock, opened the door, got inside and slammed it.

'Is that you, Daffodil?' called my mother from her bedroom.

I kicked off my shoes and crept upstairs.

'Is that you, Daffodil?'

'Yes.'

'Did you have a nice time?'

'Yes.'

I thought of poor, passionate Peter left on the doorstep, staring at the door shut in his face. It wasn't my fault, I kept telling myself.

I thought of Brian Jones in the library, I thought of the book *Sex in Marriage* at school. I slipped into bed, curled up under the covers and wondered how I was ever going to face the world again.

CHAPTER 6

So it was the dramatic society I gave up, not the Caledonian society or the youth club.

When questioned the following Monday by Rita and the rest of the group about my weekend activities, I had ready my explanation for the abrupt end of my promising romance.

'He tried to go too far,' I said. It was a complaint I had heard from the other girls.

'Oh, I know,' said Rita. 'I had the same trouble with Derek for a while. In the end I had to wear my tightest pantie-girdle until he got the message. He behaves himself now, though, cos he can see D-day on the horizon anyway.' She leaned forward confidingly. 'I nearly gave in, though. D'you know, one evening, up on the common, we were, well you know. He kept saying "Let me put it in. Go on, let me put it in." Do you know what happened?'

'No,' I said shocked and fascinated.

'There was this huge clap of thunder, just as I was about to say "Oh, all right then." I don't believe in God, but I thought He'd got me then.' She threw her head back and laughed loudly, opening her red mouth and showing all her teeth with their fillings. We all joined in the laughter, but I was thoughtful.

Had I been making too much of a fuss? I tried to visualize

the sort of girdle I would have needed to protect myself from Peter. I began to wonder if there would be a market for the Daffodil Mulligan all-enveloping chastity-belt, or would I be the only customer?

'What did you do, Daff?' Jenny asked me. The girls called me Daff, which was how I had introduced myself. They assumed my name was Daphne and I did nothing to correct them.

'I told him to lay off,' I lied glibly. 'I said I wasn't that sort of girl and if he thought I was, he was wrong and I didn't want to see him again.'

'Good for you,' said Rita. 'I reckon you handled it well.'

I reckoned that in my fantasies life could be perfect. I felt mean. They were good and caring friends.

'Men!' said Jenny. 'Why do we bother?'

'Because there's nothing else,' said Rita crisply.

'Miss West probably wouldn't agree.' said Jenny.

Everyone giggled. Miss West was in charge of the typing pool. She was middle aged and considered by the group as a frump. She wore flat shoes and tweeds and was a little superior in her manner.

'Good God! If that's the only other thing that's going, no wonder we all hang on to men like grim death!' Rita retorted. 'Who'd want to end up like that?'

Some months later we received the news that Miss West was having a passionate love affair with another director – already married with five children – with incredulity. We felt robbed of our stereotypes. I suggested that this information was propaganda put about by Miss West who was totally ashamed of herself, and the theory was received with gratitude and laughter. 'Anyway,' Rita went on, picking up the previous thread, 'he doesn't sound as if he was your type, that Peter.'

'Oh?' I was not surprised at her conclusion. What *was* my type, for heavens' sake! I put the question to the girls knowing that if they did not have the whole answer, they would at least point me in the right direction.

Rita screwed up her face and examined mine thoughtfully. 'I don't know, Daff. But that Peter – an actor – a bit, well uppity, you know.'

'Classy,' Jenny ventured. 'You're much more ordinary than that.'

'Well, you're, well, one of us,' Rita concluded, but I knew she was not quite sure, being thoroughly intimidated by my two O-levels and the knowledge that I had gone to the grammar school.

I knew what they were saying was right. I was ordinary. My background was no different from theirs in most ways. Yet I was dogged by Mother's aspirations and did not quite fit in with them. Mother would never have believed it, and I was quite relieved to realize it, after Wendy's wild excesses, that these girls' sexual morals were as rigid and strict as my own family's. Sex before marriage was forbidden and a white wedding every girl's aim. They usually married the one and only boyfriend they ever had. Going too far was frowned upon, but I was rapidly learning that they thought they could go a bit further than I thought was permissible. I adjusted my values forthwith. There was a fear and fascination about sex, as though it were something dangerous as well as exciting, to be avoided yet anticipated, but they had a sort of resignation about it. To me at the time, their attitude was that one day they would find out what a let-down it all was, how all the promises were empty; while I was convinced that when I found out about it, it was going to be the key to the Meaning of Life. I was saving myself for something marvellous. They were saving themselves up because it was the right thing to do.

'What *is* my type?' I asked them again, for they were still telling me how Peter was not my type. Either they didn't know my type or were afraid to tell me, I thought.

'There's that new clerk in Mr Forester's office,' Rita said slowly. 'I think he may be your type.'

'Bobby?' said Jenny. 'Yes – he could be your type, Daff. Sort of quiet, mature, a bit shy.'

'Oh dear,' I said and they laughed.

'No wonder you haven't had much luck,' Rita said.

'*He* wouldn't want to go too far.' Jenny said and Rita agreed.

'So long as he's not a total non-starter,' I laughed.

Rita was being thoughtful and wise again. 'Get yourself noticed, Daff. Go into Mr Forester's office. You can find an excuse. And speak to him.'

'Even if he doesn't speak to me?'

'Yeh, 'course. There was a question about that in the agony column in *Woman's Whatsit* last week. You can't leave it *all* to them, you know. You still doing those exercises, Daff?'

'Yes, of course,'

'Good. Don't stop.'

During the afternoon I took a casual peep at Bobby. The girls had given me a brief description of him so I had no difficulty in identifying him through the glass of the door of Mr Forester's office. I knew the others in there anyway. Bobby was unremarkable, really. Not tall, not dark, not handsome. He was shortish, a couple of inches taller than myself, had fairish hair and a round slightly plump and scrubbed face. These days, when I meet people who call themselves new-born Christians, I always think of Bobby with his clean and shining face. The thought went through my mind that afternoon as I strolled casually by the door, that Mother would like him. Later on, I realized that Auntie Rose would like him, too.

Meanwhile, other things were happening in my life. Mother, sick and tired of living in squalor, as she put it, had been trying for some time – years in fact – to have us moved to a council house, with a bathroom, hot water and no damp. Around this time, on grounds of health, she achieved her aim and we uprooted from the three-storey terraced house I had known as home as far back as I could remember, to a brand new council house on a brand new estate, knee high in muddy clay. Mother was overjoyed. Her health improved overnight, despite the walls running with condensation and huge fuel bills. Daddy conquered the mound of clay, putting a fine fence around what we understood was our garden. Buster had a shed for his bike and Lena and I, once the condensation had dried out, had to co-operate on a colour scheme for our shared bedroom. We had had new beds, to replace the green painted iron framed ones, for a year or two now. Daddy had had an accident at work sometime previously and the compensation money had bought several luxuries, like beds with pink bedspreads. Pink was Lena's favourite colour, and mine was blue, so I had the honour of choosing blue curtains. The whole bedroom was a compromise of alternate pink and blue choices, so that when I half-closed my eyes I had the impression that everything was a delicate shade of mauve. I suggested to Lena that we should have had everything mauve as a more harmonious compromise, but she said the colour did not suit her complexion.

As a result of this co-operation over the new bedroom or perhaps just because we were older, Lena was fifteen and I eighteen, I began to see Lena more as a friend than the bloody nuisance I had always thought her to be. I might have been missing Wendy's company too. Since we had moved, I saw her less and less.

Anyway, lying in bed at night, Lena and I would sometimes talk. She would tell me about her exploits at school, I would give a vivid, exaggerated account of the lives of the girls at work. Lena was very interested in Rita's forthcoming wedding.

'How long is it now?' she asked one night.

'Four weeks. The invitations have gone out. I've got one. I don't know what to wear.'

'You'll get something new,' she said.

'I'll have to. I'm waiting to see the bridesmaids. She's had to put it up to seven. They're going to be the colours of the rainbow.'

'Do you want to get married, Daff?'

'Yes, of course. I don't want to be left on the shelf, a crabby old spinster.'

'Do spinsters have to be old and crabby? Think of Miss Davies, our English teacher. She's ever so nice. She's not a crabby old spinster,' Lena said.

'Oh, has she got married, then?'

'No. She's – well,' giggled Lena leaning across the chasm between the two beds. Even in the darkness I could feel her laughter. 'She's one of those.'

'One of what?'

'Them! Bent, queer.' Her voice lowered. 'A lesbian.'

To my mind, the word contained more accusation than information. 'Don't be ridiculous. She looks quite normal to me.'

'Doesn't make any difference. Lots of them are quite normal to look at.'

'How do *you* know?'

'About Miss Davies? People know at school. She doesn't hide it. She's got a lover,' Lena smacked her lips and if I could have seen her expression, her eyes would have rolled. 'We talk about things like that at school. Didn't you?'

'Of course. But we didn't have your avid interest. You seem mightily interested, if you ask me.'

Lena giggled. 'I've got a boyfriend.'

Brief silence. 'Ooh!' I said. 'For heaven's sake don't tell Mother. She'll be wild.'

'She knows.'

'Knows? What did she say?'

'She said I'd probably end up having to get married at eighteen and I'd have lots of kids.'

'Will you?'

'No. I'm going to qualify as a teacher. If I get my O-levels this year. I'm going into the sixth form. I'm insisting. Mother can't stop me. Willie is in my form.'

Bleakness swept over me. It was not jealousy, I promise, just saddness that I, trying so hard to be good in order to get my own way, never got it, and was not considered to be good either. Good luck to Lena, I thought. Especially with a boyfriend named Willie.

'Willie!' I sputtered. 'Willie!'

Lena protested mildly at my rudeness.

'Daff,' she said, 'Daff, what happened to Peter?'

I stopped spluttering and acted mysteriously. 'You don't ask questions like that, Lena. Besides . . . and here I made a decision, not just any old decision but a Big Decision that altered the course of my life, 'I've met somebody else, now. I think I've met Mr Right'.

'Ooh Daff! Really? You gonna get married?'

'I don't know about that. I'm still at the stage of worshipping him from afar.'

'Do you know his name?'

'Oh, yes. Listen to this. His name is Bobby Wright!'

Lena giggled again. 'I won't tell Mother,' she said.

'You can if you like,' I said airily, thinking a gradual filtering of information via Lena might be an appropriate way of avoiding Mother's dreadful prophesies of sexual downfall. 'He hasn't asked me out yet. But he will. He will.'

The next day I took trouble to be in the queue at the cafeteria next to Bobby. In reply to my complaints first about the weather, then about the queue, then about the food, he nodded, smiled and said 'Yes.'

I peered over his shoulder towards where my friends were sitting, curious to see if they had noticed me next to Bobby. I waved ostentatiously and Rita lifted a hand in reply.

'They're my friends,' I explained to Bobby. 'We're all from Sales. You're in Mr Forester's office, aren't you?'

Again, the nod, the smile and the reply. 'Yes.'

Jenny had been wrong when she said he was a bit shy. He was extremely shy. Emboldened by advantage socially, I said, 'Who do you sit with at lunch time?'

'Anybody,' he said. 'I usually read.' He patted his jacket pocket stuffed with a paperback novel.

'Join us,' I said, really getting the hang of this. 'You know Rita, don't you?'

'Yes,' he said.

And that is how Bobby joined us for lunch that day and most days afterwards. He didn't say much but ate his lunch with a fixed grin and short replies to our statements and questions. He left before we did, which gave us an opportunity to analyse him.

'He's very bookish,' was Jenny's verdict.

'Definitely your sort,' said Rita. 'But definitely not mine.'

'The strong and silent type.' said Betty.

'He's okay,' I said casually.

Two days later, after lunch, when the others had left – in rather a hurry, I thought, – Bobby asked me if I would like to go to the cinema the following Saturday. He was rather pink when he asked me and didn't look at me but stared at his plate and the remains of semolina pudding. He told me later he hated semolina and had ordered it in a state of confusion because of what he planned to do. Rita told me, after the weekend, that she had suggested to Bobby that morning that if he was interested she was reasonably sure that I would be willing to go out with him if he could summon up the courage to ask me.

The date was an unremarkable but comfortable event. We went to the cinema, then for a walk and asked questions about each other. He walked me home, said good-night at the gate and off he went. No kisses, no hand-holding, no demands, but a promise of a date next week.

I decided I was going to marry Bobby.

I reported back to Lena, who reported back to Mother, who issued mild warnings but to my surprise seemed pleased that I had another boyfriend and wanted me to bring him home to tea some day soon. As I was quite anxious not to put Bobby off, I delayed this invitation for as long as I could.

Bobby was a pleasant, easy companion, very polite and amenable, but not very au fait with the pleasures of the world, like pubs, theatres, restaurants. Most of our outings consisted of walks together, the occasional film and, later on, tea at his mother's. He lived the other side of the town from us, right on the edge in fact, with a back garden facing fields. Bobby's father, on my every visit, seemed to feel it was his duty to give me a conducted tour of the garden, and I learned some useful tips from him, as well as arriving home on most Saturday nights bearing gifts of runner beans, cabbages, tomatoes, bunches of flowers and pots of blackcurrant jam, made by Mrs Wright with blackcurrants grown by her husband.

Bobby's family, like himself, were quiet, old-fashioned and didn't believe in modern aids to living like washing-machines, double knitting wool, drip-dry non-iron fabrics or sliced bread. They lived and worked hard and simply and I admired their detachment from life and obvious enjoyment of their own values. In my mind I described them as peasants and this was by no means disparaging.

Bobby's father was a gardener and his mother did cleaning at a big house a mile or so down the lane. There was a younger sister, Barbara, twelve years younger than Bobby, at fourteen, who was a slight oddity too, plump and seemingly slow, but apparently very clever at school. She too worked hard and enjoyed it. Like us, they had no television, and like us, until recently, no bathroom and only an outside toilet. It was this, above all, that gave me a real affinity with Bobby. He and I, I felt, were at odds with the rest of the world.

Barbara seemed to resent me at first, but then became very friendly, especially if I tried to help her with her homework. Unlike the girls at work, who were intimidated by my two O-levels, Barbara was contemptuous and told me I should have worked harder.

Bobby had left school at sixteen, worked in an office in the town until he changed his job to come to our place. I learned that he had never had a girlfriend before, that he enjoyed reading and collecting coins. Apart from telling each other about our past lives, we talked mostly about books and about the state of the world, which we both agreed was an awful place apart from the cosy niche we were making for the pair of us.

Inevitably, I had to broach the subject of Bobby meeting my parents. This was about two months after our initial meeting and we had now reached the holding hands stage. It was a mild autumn Saturday afternoon and we were wandering, hand in hand, down the lanes on the outskirts of the town.

'My mother wants to meet you, Bobby,' I said. 'She wants to see who it is I spend my Saturday afternoons with.'

'I'm not looking forward to meeting your mother, Daff,' he said, 'not after all the things you've told me about her.'

'Oh, she's all right really,' I said. 'I exaggerate, and anyway, she'll be anxious to make a good impression.'

'So will I,' said Bobby earnestly.

'That's all right,' I said lightly. 'I'm anxious that you both make a good impression. And Daddy'll be there. He's OK. Shall I say next Saturday?'

'Yes,' said Bobby.

'There's just one thing,' I began. 'I have a confession to

make. My name is not Daphne, as everyone thinks.'

'What is it, then?'

'It's Daffodil,' I admitted dramatically.

'Oh, is it?' Bobby clearly did not understand my sensitivity about my name nor the reason for my revelation.

'My parents are quite likely to call me Daffodil, or Daffie,' I explained.

'Oh, that's all right,' he said. 'My name's not Robert. It's just Bobby. Look, it must be getting late. Those cows are going in. It must be milking time.'

'Milking time?'

He looked at his watch. I looked at the cattle. They were certainly not going to be milked. They had no udders. They were heiffers. I looked at Bobby – fondly, of course. How had I described him to Lena the other night? Out of this world!

CHAPTER 7

For Rita's wedding I bought a beautiful red chiffon dress. Mother thought it ostentatious and made some joke about me being a scarlet woman, but at that time the significance was lost on me.

Rita's wedding was a lavish affair. All her friends at work had been invited and so had Bobby, though when that scheme had been perpetrated, I was not aware. To my delight, I found myself sitting next to Bobby in the church, with Betty, Jenny and her fiancé and the others. If this doesn't give him ideas, I thought, I don't know what will. And I was certain Rita had been of the same mind.

I knew I looked stupendous in my red chiffon dress and black wide-brimmed hat. I did not dress up very often, having neither the will nor the occasion and my choice of clothes for every day was very plain and unfussy – conservative was the word. So I knew the impact I made when I pulled out all the stops was the greater for its unexpectedness. In fact, when I saw Bobby stop in the aisle, as though to retreat rather than join me in the pew, I wondered briefly if I had gone too far.

'You look nice,' Bobby said eventually.

I whispered back, 'Thank you,' by now prepared for his understatements. Jenny and Betty's reactions had been totally gratifying.

'Blimey!' said Betty, 'You look like a film star!'

'Didn't recognize you,' said Jenny. 'You look fantastic.'

There was a flurry of activity in the porch and a ripple went through the church. The bride had arrived. Great chords bellowed from the organ. Everyone stood up. My stomach turned over with excitement and my eyes filled with tears as Rita went by. I looked at Jenny and I could see she felt the same. Rita had made it! Thank goodness! Yes, I know what the agony columns in women's magazines say about marriage being a beginning and happily ever after is a myth, but Jenny and I both knew that Rita had achieved something that we also were working towards.

The rainbow bridesmaids looked lovely and indigo can look surprisingly good in satin, especially if kept among the other six colours. Rita of course was beautiful in an elaborate white lace dress that had cost her the earth and of which I caught only a glimpse because I was gazing at her face under the veil, and she looked, well, radiant, as she was supposed to do.

I shared a hymn book with Bobby and sang lustily. Bobby kept knocking my hat askew as he leaned over the pages, and kept apologizing and I kept saying 'It's all right.'

Then the service was over, Rita came down the aisle, head and veil thrown back triumphantly and everyone poured out of church.

'Isn't it all lovely!' I said to Bobby.

'Yes,' he said.

I linked my arm in his because I knew no one would be ashamed to be seen with me today. I think he was a bit self-conscious, though, because people kept looking at me. In fact, several times during the day I checked my appearance against my reflection in mirrors, doors and windows because I was not used to so much non-verbal adulation and I wondered if something was wrong, like my petticoat showing or a hem coming undone. But no, nothing was amiss.

The reception in the church hall was like nothing I had ever experienced. The food and wine were on a scale I had seen only in films. I must make it clear, too, that I had never had an opportunity to drink so much alcohol! At home we had drinks only at Christmas, and that was at the most, two bottles of wine shared among the family and stretched over the whole festive season.

After two glasses of wine, I was unusually happy. I felt confident and witty and was encouraged by the laughter of Jenny and her fiancé and Betty, and Bobby as I chattered, made jokes and held their attention. Bobby sat on my hat and apologized but I just laughed.

Then the band struck up.

'Oh, Bobby, can you dance?' I said, hanging on to his arm. I fully expected him to say 'yes.' But he stepped back, shook his head and said, 'No.'

'Oh!' I wailed. 'Surely you can! Not just a little bit?'

After all my time with the Caledonian society (which at this point I was about to leave), I was a passable dancer and enjoyed it thoroughly, and now was not a bit hesitant about moving out on to the dance floor. I had had a few lessons in ballroom dancing at school and felt I could soon pick up the steps again with a decent partner. But Bobby was not going to be even an indecent partner.

With the Caledonian society behind me and an unprecendented amount of alcohol inside me, I could have danced a paso doble that day. In fact, I might well have done; I don't recall exactly what I did dance. I do know that a man nearby, hearing my protestations, asked me to dance. He was middle aged, hardly spoke, and breathed alcohol fumes heavily through his nostrils. And could dance! He was a wonderful partner. He asked me to dance again – and again, and again. I knew we were attracting attention. In fact, at times, we were the only people dancing. Every so often he would mutter inarticulately, vanish briefly, only to reappear with a drink for himself and one for me.

I also made an embarrassing discovery. I had never before danced so closely to a man not wearing a sporran. What I experienced with this, nameless, man was a slight shock. There it was, large as life, the thing I had spent a great deal of my life pursuing with mixed reverence and fear, and the object of my obsession. I had never been so close to one. And he was not ashamed of it. That amazed me. Drink dulled my embarrassment. So that's the size of it, I thought.

I vaguely remember Rita and her husband leaving for their honeymoon as I was complaining to Bobby that I felt a bit dizzy.

'I'm not surprised,' he commented, and indicated that I should sit down next to him which I did.

'I'll get you some coffee,' Betty said. 'That's what you need. Coffee, strong and black,'

'Thanks,' I said feebly. I looked at Bobby, who was not looking at me and suddenly began to feel very guilty. Was he annoyed with me?

Betty came back with the coffee, which I drank.

'I feel sick,' I said.

I could hear a conversation going on across me, or over me and certainly about me, between Bobby and Betty. Bobby was being advised to take me outside, get a taxi and take me home, get me some more coffee. I think Bobby did all of these things, some of them more than once. He seemed to be talking a lot, he was very concerned about me and said something about being unkind dancing all evening with that man and marrying me. But all I could think of was the routine I rehearsed in my mind – getting into the taxi, getting out again, getting indoors and upstairs to my bed without Mother or Daddy seeing me. It was not that I could not remember what had happened, but that I felt too ill to dwell on what was being said. I remember Bobby, more than once during the evening, kissing me with a moderate passion, but I was in no state to appreciate it.

I kept telling Bobby I was all right and, hanging on to my squashed hat, staggered as quietly as I could out of the taxi, into the house, up the stairs and on to my bed.

Oh – the relief!

'I can see you've enjoyed yourself,' came Lena's voice from the bed across the room.

I groaned in reply. My hat fell from my fingers on to the floor.

'Shall I get Mother?'

'For God's sake, no!' I feel sick.' I staggered off the bed, stepping on to the hat and squashing it again, and stumbled as quietly as I could to the bathroom.

When I returned Lena asked me if I felt better.

'I think so,' I said.

'Did you enjoy yourself?' she asked.

'I'm not sure.'

'You'd better get your dress off, or you'll spoil it,' she advised.

'In a minute. In a minute.'

'I know what you need,' she said. 'Get your dress off and get into bed quickly.'

She crept out of the room and downstairs to return a few minutes later with a glass of something fizzy which she instructed me to drink. I snuggled down into bed, thanking her.

'How was Bobby?' she asked.

I wanted to go to sleep 'Fine,' I murmured. 'I think I might marry him.'

Even in my battered and bleary state, I expected a response to that.

'Wendy's in the family way,' she announced.

Lena never could keep a secret and it must have been very

frustrating for her that night that my response to her news was to drift quietly off to sleep. And when she woke up the next morning, the information to the forefront of her mind, I was still asleep. The rest of the family had gone to Mass and left me lying there, so I knew that they knew that I had had too much to drink the previous evening. I also knew that, in Mother's eyes, drink was the next evil after sex, and, in fact, often led to it, so my first thoughts concerned her reaction and not the fact that my brain in my skull felt like a loose nut in its shell, nor that I had been proposed to by Bobby, nor that Wendy, according to Lena, had fallen foul of sex.

I decided to get up and go to the next Mass, leaving the house before the family returned, and instead of going straight home, I would go round to Wendy's afterwards to find out if what Lena had said was true.

On the way to church I did wonder briefly if getting drunk was a mortal sin, but decided it was not because a lot of Catholics seemed to do it and anyway, I didn't do it on purpose. And I didn't want to do it again, either. According to my mother, although she put it rather more obliquely, a lot of Catholics had sex a lot and she knew because some families were larger than average – and even in marriage this was not desirable. I knew better, however, having studied the CTS pamphlets thoroughly and a little tingle of excitement mingled with fear went through me as I realized that, if Bobby had meant what he said last night – and that must be established – I would soon know all about sex in practice as well as in theory and we would be able to indulge in it legitimately to our heart's content.

As I approached Wendy's house, I began to have doubts about the nature of my mission, but my head was throbbing somewhat so the attractions of a cup of coffee and curiosity to be satisfied were the spurs.

Wendy's mother answered the door. She did not seem too pleased to see me and at first I thought it was disapproval of me, as if I had done something wrong. Then I realized that she thought I had come to gloat. I mentioned my hangover to prove that I was not perfect either.

Wendy made some coffee in the kitchen and we exchanged awkward pleasantries for a while. At least, I felt awkward. I was amazed that Wendy showed no shame, indeed, was even a little superior. There was a barrier between us at first. Wendy's mother hovered and did not go, even when we finally mentioned The Subject.

'I saw Lena in the town yesterday,' Wendy explained. 'And I told her. I told her to tell you.'

'Don't you mind people knowing?' I asked.

'Not some people. But I'm going away soon. I didn't want to just disappear.'

'Where are you going?'

'To my grandmother's. Then I'll stay there for a while and see what happens.'

'Are you going to keep it?'

Mrs Robinson, behind me, overheard and snorted. 'As if I'd let my own grandchild be adopted! As if I'd do that to my own daughter!'

I thought of my mother. 'You're lucky,' I said.

'Lucky! Of course she's lucky,' Mrs Robinson said, 'Lucky but silly.'

She took me upstairs to her room, much to my relief, for there were questions I wanted to ask her which I dare not in front of her mother.

'Mummy is a bit put out,' said Wendy. 'But she's been very good really. And Daddy. After all, I'm the one whose got to have it.'

I sympathized but could see that Wendy was in her element.

'When is it going to be?' I asked and for the first time allowed my gaze to settle on her stomach. She noticed and patted the slight bulge proudly.

‘In March,’ she said. I did a quick calculation and thought, ‘Light summer nights – I see.’

Wendy started chatting about the knitting she was doing and the baby clothes and equipment she had bought. I admired some extravagant lacy little garments then said to her ‘Who was it?’ tentatively.

‘Why, Brian Jones, of course,’ she said. I felt a bit odd, like I had had a narrow escape or something.

‘Does he know? Didn’t you want to get married?’ I persisted.

‘He knows all right. He’s scarpered off to somewhere in Africa, would you believe? Marry him? I thought so at first, but he didn’t like the idea. I’m glad really. I think I shall enjoy looking after a baby without having to share it with a man.’

‘But that’s a terrible thing to say!’ I was shocked.

Wendy shrugged.

‘But how did it happen?’

‘What do you mean, how did it happen? You were the one who gave *me* all the information, if I remember!’

‘I don’t mean that,’ I said struggling to understand and to throw off a feeling that this might, in the final analysis, be all my fault. ‘What I mean is,’ I hesitated, because this was an unforgivable intrusion, ‘how and when and where did you, you know, do It?’

‘In the back of his car.’ Wendy said.

I wanted to know more, but was afraid to ask. In the back of a car did not sound either romantic or comfortable. There was a silence. Then I asked, ‘Is it – you know – nice?’

Wendy’s shrug was dismissive not only of the question but of the notion behind it. ‘It’s nothing,’ she said.

‘Nothing?’ I repeated, startled.

‘Nothing,’ she said.

‘You mean you didn’t enjoy it?’

‘Oh, it was, well, mildly pleasant at times.’

This was bad news indeed. After I’d decided not to be a

nun, the whole of my life had been geared towards being initiated into these secrets, these indescribable pleasures, and finding the right man with whom to indulge, share, be transported. And here was Wendy saying it was nothing . . .

She couldn't have been doing it right, I thought. Perhaps Brian Jones wasn't the right man for her. Perhaps she hadn't loved him enough, or properly. How could you do it right in the back of a car?

'Perhaps Brian Jones wasn't the right person for you,' I ventured. 'Perhaps it would have been different with someone else.'

Wendy took a final swipe at my dreams, illusions, fantasies, prayers. 'Brian Jones was not the first,' she said.

I wandered home in a daze. I tried to focus on Bobby and his proposal, but I was not too happy about that because it seemed so vague. I needed to check it out with him. I was glad I had not told Wendy about it for I think I had fully intended to do so when I set out to see her.

But her attitude to sex shocked me. Where was love? I asked myself. She didn't deserve to enjoy it. And look at the situation she was in now. Brian Jones was a brute. Thank goodness Bobby was a gentle, considerate sort of man. Our relationship would be different. I would devote my all to him, he would be my life's work. Bobby and I would have all the right values. We would not be like Wendy, Rita, Jenny and their men, or even like my parents. We would be totally honest, trusting and virtuous, not cynical and grasping.

I arrived home to find a smoky haze throughout the house and the smell of food, some of it burnt. It made me feel sick.

'There you are!' Mother exlaimed as I walked in the back door. 'Where have you been?'

'I've been to see Wendy,' I said, not knowing whether I preferred to be castigated for that, or for drinking too much the previous day

Mother lowered her voice to a whisper and I wondered why. 'I don't know why you bother with a girl like that.' Then she raised her voice and sounded utterly charming. 'There's a visitor waiting to see you in the front room.'

It was Bobby!

Bobby had come round to find out how I was. I was so thrilled until I remembered how I had been. All that drink, all that dancing and the things I had said! It wasn't that I couldn't remember the next day, rather it was that I preferred not to do so. No wonder Bobby had proposed! At one point I had thrown myself on to his lap, put my arms round his neck and said 'Hallo, lover boy!' Yes, I really must check out on this proposal business.

Bobby stayed to lunch. He did not eat much. His mother was a much better cook than mine could ever dream to be. I ate little, too. Then we went out to walk from my house to his house where we were expected for tea. This was some distance, right across the town, as the crow flies, and even further as Bobby walked, round the edge of the town. Bobby walked everywhere. It was as though he had a conscientious objection to the invention and use of the wheel. Very far back, was Bobby. He didn't believe in anything artificial.

We held hands once we were out of sight of our road. We held an inquest on yesterday's events. I apologized for drinking too much.

'I'm not used to it, you see,' I explained. 'I didn't realize how it was affecting me.'

'I'm not used to it, either,' he said. 'I don't think I'd have had the courage to ask you what I did if I hadn't had two glasses of wine.'

'What did you ask me?' I teased, noticing that his face had gone pink right to the tips of his ears.

'I'll ask you again if you repeat what you said,' he said craftily.

I stopped walking and went hot. What had I said? The

most outrageous thing had surely been to call him 'lover boy'. I looked around. We were in a lane in open country. What on earth had I said? Had it been an open invitation to seduction? If so, was I safe here?

'What particular saying of mine had you in mind?' I inquired warily.

'Don't you remember?' It had not occurred to him that I thought I might have forgotten something. 'When you took a flying leap towards me, threw yourself into my arms and . . .'

'Oh, that!' I laughed. 'I thought you meant what I said when you sat on my hat.'

'Oh. I didn't hear that,' said Bobby. And it was just as well.

'OK,' I said. 'You stand back by that gate – no sit on the ground.'

'I'd rather do that. You're a big girl,' he said, but I forgave him instantly.

He sat on the grass by the gate. I sank on to his lap, put my arms around his neck and said huskily into his ear, 'Hello, lover boy!'

'Hello,' he said. 'If you're going to dance with other men all the time I can see I'm going to have to marry you so's I can say you're mine and then forbid it.'

'Oh!' I said, 'You're so masterful!' and we collapsed into laughter because the way he said it was not really masterful at all.

Then he kissed me and I kissed him back and we had a chaste little cuddle before setting out for tea at the Wrights.

CHAPTER 8

Bobby and I decided that we would be 'unofficially' engaged for a few weeks. This meant I could prepare my parents gently, he could prepare his parents and he would buy me a locket to wear on a chain round my neck and I would put a photograph of each of us in it.

Among the girls at work, this was the routine. If you were unofficially engaged, you kept it secret for a while but, of course, told your best friends and got their advice on what sort of ring you would choose. Usually, the unofficial fiancé was persuaded to buy a locket, only silver, but of enormous symbolic value among the friends. If a girl wore a locket, you knew she had a boyfriend and it would not be long before she became engaged to him.

The official engagement was something different. This was public, relatives were informed, announcements appeared in the local paper, the date of the wedding set, the ring worn, the boss told, and was in some cases celebrated with an elaborate party. I knew we wouldn't get a party. My mother was not too keen on people enjoying themselves.

Bobby and I were going to be officially engaged at Christmas. We spent many a Saturday afternoon gazing in jewellers' shops and I hoped to have a sapphire and diamond ring.

The girls at work were overjoyed when I told them, though, Rita didn't know until two weeks later when she returned from her honeymoon.

Lena, of course, could be relied upon to drop a hint to Mother.

'Are you going to marry him?' Mother asked me one evening the following week as we were washing up. I smiled and turned away.

'I might,' I said mysteriously.

'When? Next Easter?'

I was astounded. 'Give us a chance,' I said, spinning round. 'We don't know each other that well yet.'

'You will by next Easter,' Mother said.

'And suppose by next Easter I discovered I didn't want to marry him?' I demanded. 'What's the hurry?'

'I'd just like to see you settled,' she said.

'Well, you just be patient like a good mummy and you'll see me settled about this time next year.'

Mother sighed. 'I don't believe in long engagements,' she said.

I could see what was on her mind, it had been on her mind for several years, probably since about the time I started wearing a bra. She wanted to see me safely tamed in marriage, or rather, my passions safely tamed in marriage before I slipped up like Wendy had done. She was concerned, not for me, not for any baby I might have, but for her reputation.

'You make me sick!' I said, flinging down the tea-towel. 'You're only worried that I might have to get married. Well, let me tell you, I'm a respectable girl. I don't know about you.'

'So was I,' said Mother.

'Well, I am. And I intend to go on being.'

But oh, it became so difficult! So near, I thought, yet so far.

Bobby and I saw each other every evening except Monday. Most of the time we spent either at my house or at his house. Sometimes we went for trips out, usually involving a lot of walking, mostly in the countryside, sometimes we saw a film. Mother began to complain that Bobby was always in the house and she objected to getting meals for him, but I could never understand her objections, because the evenings Bobby wasn't there, I wasn't there either. To me it was as broad as it was long.

On Monday evenings Bobby stayed at home with his mother who, in my opinion, was a little possessive of him. She didn't think I should have all his time. Having left the Caledonian society and the church youth club, I now needed something else to do so I joined the church choir, newly formed and crying out for members. We had a new young priest in the parish and his ideas were also new and young. As choir master he enlisted the services of a young music teacher from the grammar school, called Sebastian Power, and I found myself enthralled at the idea of mixing socially with the sort of people who, a few years earlier, had been superior to me. Sebastian was good-looking as well as talented and I learned a lot from him. As well as music for Mass and the psalms, he taught us other pieces for Christmas, some of them very sophisticated. His wife, Dolores, was also in the choir and she and I were the stable core of altos. She was beautiful, with short dark hair, large brown eyes and always laughing, not at people, but at life. She inspired confidence in everyone and was always encouraging. I looked forward to Monday evenings tremendously.

After a while, when the weather got colder, we moved choir practice from the church to the presbytery. This was much more congenial. Apart from sitting in cosy armchairs round a fire, there was coffee and biscuits afterwards and Father Daly, whom we soon began to call Father Terry, would join us and we would sit until very late, talking and putting the world and the church to rights. At these sessions I began to rethink my attitude to the church and allowed myself to question a lot of things that hitherto I had taken as immutable. I even found myself talking, on one occasion, about my mother and how difficult I found her, and how angry I was with her at times.

'I know what you're at,' said Father Terry. 'You want to get your version in first, so that when I meet her my views will be prejudiced.'

I laughed. If I couldn't be liked for loving my mother, I would be liked for my honesty. 'There might be some truth in that. Once she threatened to bring me down to the presbytery to get Father Wilkins to give me a good talking to. Now I'm doing it to her.'

Sebastian was amused. 'You shouldn't be in such awe of authority,' he said.

'Shouldn't I?' I said, bemused and wondering if he gave such advice to his pupils.

'Even priests sin, Daff,' said Dolores.

'Are you sure?' I asked horrified, and everyone laughed. It was as though they knew the thought that had flashed through my mind – the popular view is that sin is synonymous with sex, and I was not immune from this. Even in the church I could not hide my preoccupation.

Rita returned from her honeymoon in Spain looking tanned and plumper. We were all pleased to have her back in the office because she was such a live-wire. Also, we wanted to know whether she liked being married. There was a post mortem at lunch time.

Rita sat like a queen entertaining her court, her wedding ring and engagement ring something of a burden now they were on the same finger – she kept playing with them.

'I can't get used to being Mrs,' she laughed. 'It makes me feel so old. There was all this post on the doormat when we got back, addressed to Mr and Mrs Brown. I've got mixed feelings about that after being Smith for twenty years.'

'Did they know you were on your honeymoon at the hotel?' asked Jenny.

'Know? Confetti was falling out of our clothes like snow!' Rita laughed. Then she turned to me and Bobby: 'Well, I'm surprised at your news,' she said in a low voice, because the engagement was unofficial. 'Congratulations! I hope I'll get invited to the wedding.'

'Of course,' I said, looking at Bobby for confirmation.

I guessed that Rita wanted to talk in a private fashion to the other girls, so I drew Bobby away and we went off for yet another walk.

Later I saw Rita for a confidential chat in the office.

'I must say,' she grinned, 'I'm surprised at you and Bobby. I didn't expect anything to happen so soon.'

'I'm not as slow as you think I am,' I said.

'Neither is Bobby,' she said.

I hesitated. 'Rita,' I began. 'It is worth getting married, isn't it?'

'Why, do you have doubts?'

'Oh, no!'

'It's normal to have doubts. Don't you love him, then?'

'Oh yes! We love each other very much.' I wanted to add that our love was special, different and was not entangled with status symbols like washing-machines and refrigerators. As much as I liked Rita and the other girls, I judged them to be very materialistic.

'Well, you really ought to ask someone who's been married more than a fortnight,' Rita said. 'But yes, I do like it. I like having someone special of my own, I like being special to someone, I like doing things for him. I look forward to going home to him tonight. I like the idea of being Mrs – it's important. People respect you if you've got a man behind you.'

'And what about . . .' I began, desperate to know her answer, reasonably sure that she wouldn't mind the question. 'You know – making love?'

'Oh that!' she said dismissively, and my heart sank. 'Don't you get expecting too much from that. It's not like in books and films. It's OK, though, I suppose. But, you know, most men don't know all that much about it,' she added mysteriously.

That last remark bothered me for some time. Not just the rest of the afternoon, during which I was dying to ask for clarification. I dared not. I thought I had intruded enough.

I went home feeling uneasy but unable to explain to myself why, nor even to connect my low spirits with my conversation with Rita.

Bobby and I had planned one of our rare visits to the cinema that evening, so eating my tea and getting ready to go out were a rush. Lena, being awkward I am sure, occupied the bathroom for an unnecessary length of time; she was not usually so fussy about her appearance and cleanliness. As she came out of the bathroom, I jostled her to get in. She resisted. There was a slight tussle and she pulled the chain of my locket. It broke. I snapped. I shouted and screamed and bellowed at her. This time, I was convinced, my protests were justified. This time Lena would get into trouble. She had broken the locket chain that Bobby had bought me. Mother liked Bobby. She would sympathize.

But no, I was in trouble for making such a fuss.

'Honestly, Daffodil,' said Mother, who had limped up the stairs to find out what was going on. 'It's a simple break – it can easily be mended. There's no need to create such a disturbance in the family.'

'But she broke it. Deliberately, I expect.' I stamped my foot, tears welling in my eyes. 'Poor Bobby spent his hard-earned money on this for me. He'll be ever so cross that she's broken it.'

‘Oh, Daffodil. It was an accident. He’ll understand. There is no need at all for the fuss you’re making. Really, Daffodil, you are so unreasonable at times. Now stop. You’re disturbing the whole family.’

‘I?’ I stabbed my finger at my chest and squeaked ‘I? *I* didn’t break it!’

Instead of getting angry again, Mother went quieter and shook her head. ‘This long engagement is obviously a strain on you. It’s not good for your glands.’

I gasped. I was outraged.

‘The sooner you get married,’ Mother added, ‘the better. We can’t all suffer for your problems.’

Then she limped downstairs. Lena sniggered at me. I slammed the bathroom door, got ready quickly and sobbed all the way to Bobby’s arms.

Bobby and I became officially engaged two days before Christmas. I was given a sparkling diamond and sapphire ring which, to me, as well as being a symbol of Bobby’s love, was a sign that I, Daffodil Mulligan, was like other people, could conform and fade into society and not fear lonely spinsterhood, not continue living in the bosom of the family as their problem. Bobby was my knight in shining armour who was going to take me away from ‘all this’, whatever ‘all this’ was. I was no end grateful to Bobby.

To celebrate this momentous occasion, Mother invited Bobby and his parents and Barbara to tea. I was apprehensive about this but Bobby tried to reassure me: his parents were shy, retiring people who would not expect elaborate hospitality. I had to explain to Bobby that he had not reassured me at all. My mother was a powerful woman with an inferiority complex who would not hesitate to try and make an impression on the least sophisticated to gain a point in her own eyes.

‘The hospitality,’ I explained to Bobby, ‘will be elaborate

as far as the frills are concerned. But there will be rock cakes that are inedible, as usual, a sponge cake like rock cakes and fruit and jelly swamped in evaporated milk. And she'll talk in a loud voice, but never finish a sentence because she thinks that's posh.'

Bobby smiled, gave me a hug and told me not to worry. But I did and I was more than justified. Mother was worse than I had predicted. Lena and Barbara glowered at each other because they were at rival grammar schools. Daddy and Bobby's father spent most of the time in the other room, at the window, gazing out, talking desperately about gardens on the shortest day of the year. I think Bobby was as relieved as I was when at seven o'clock all the Wrights and myself were bundled into a taxi and driven back to their own home. Mrs Wright said my mother was a very nice woman but I noticed the relief with which she shut her own front door behind her. I felt the same.

Working in the same environment as someone with whom one is passionately in love can be difficult. The temptation to seize a quick cuddle in a dark corner gradually becomes a temptation to indulge in a long passionate embrace, with reprimands on return or discovery as a result. So I decided to do the noble thing and change my job. After all, as I had said to Bobby, his job was more important than mine. I did not expect to work that long after our marriage. I found a congenial little job as manageress of a dry-cleaner's and, despite Mother's disapproval in the face of my unwillingness to explain the change, and missing the company of Rita, Betty and Jenny, quite enjoyed the work. Often Bobby would come and sit at the back of the shop on Saturday until I closed, so I minded the Saturday working less than I might have done. Our long, passionate embraces were kept to evenings and weekends. At first, I had found these long, passionate embraces something of an embarrassment for the same reason as I had been, initially, embarrassed by dancing closely with the nameless man at Rita's wedding. But the embarrassment wore off as I began to see Bobby's response as a compliment. Anyway, I told myself, I shall have to make friends with this thing one day.

I was very eager to make our marriage an extremely happy one, so I began to watch married couples with a critical eye. I did not include my own parents in the survey as I was convinced that my mother had completely the wrong idea. She dominated Daddy almost totally. I observed Bobby's parents and was not too impressed by what I saw there. His father hardly conversed with the rest of the family. This was not for any reason of antagonism but appeared to be due to his accepted superiority in the household. He would ask what the time was, was it raining, or what time tea was, but not discuss the news on the radio, Barbara's education or where Bobby and I were going to live, this latter being a problem that Bobby and I, my parents, Rita and the group and choir members discussed repeatedly and at length.

For the ideal married couple I looked to Sebastian and Dolores. They communicated so easily and readily, not only by words but by smiles and glances. If Dolores and I were muttering quietly when we should not have been during choir practice, he was not afraid to tell us both off in the same manner, and Dolores accepted it. I admired Sebastian's patience, his good humour and thought that, Bobby might in ten years' time, be a bit like him.

Dolores was lovely. She took a great interest in my wedding plans. She said she believed in marriage and was very happy. I wanted to be like her. In fact, on one or two occasions, I talked so much about Sebastian and Dolores that Bobby became a bit annoyed and went quiet.

Bobby, not being a Catholic, was required, during the period of the engagement, to have the Roman Catholic faith explained to him by Father Terry, so that he would know what he was taking on in marrying me. At first Bobby was very reluctant, for he wasn't the sort of person to welcome new experiences and ideas with open arms, but he soon grew to like Father Terry and to enjoy the sessions. I went along too. Father Terry's informality and his humour, together with the information he imparted, made this quite an experience for me.

'For instance,' said Father Terry one evening, 'it is not Christian teaching, much as many Catholics and others think it is, that the body and soul are separate, that the body is evil and the soul good. That is a Greek idea that has infiltrated and is a heresy really. The Hebrew teaching, if you read the Old Testament, is that the body and soul are not separate and that the body is good. That, then, makes sex a gift of God, not something not quite nice.'

I blushed. Bobby stared at his feet.

'I didn't know that,' I murmured.

'Many people don't,' said Father Terry. 'When you next pick up your Bible, read the Song of Songs.'

'The Song of Songs?' I repeated. 'What's that?'

'One of the most erotic pieces of poetry ever written. It's in the Old Testament. Look it up. Of course, some translators have, in their puritanism, taken the more specific words out and substituted something innocuous for them. For instance, navel isn't really a navel at all. Read it. You'll enjoy it.'

I think my long passionate embrace with Bobby as we said good-night that evening, was a little shorter than usual.

When I was in bed, I looked up the Song of Songs. I was amazed. I showed it to Lena. She was amazed. Mother came in and wanted to know what we were reading.

'Oh, nothing, really,' said Lena. 'Just this very sexy poem in the Bible.'

Mother said we had disgusting minds. I just thought to myself that it was no wonder people did not enjoy sex if they had that attitude.

The wedding was arranged for July. Mother found us a tiny but cosy little flat in the town that was to be vacant from June and suggested we brought the date forward, but we agreed to wait until July. Mother's co-operation in the plans for our forthcoming marriage bordered on interference, but I was quite happy to let it be that way for I had anticipated disapproval and even hindrance. Bobby did not resent her avid interest, so I accepted it.

Then, one Sunday afternoon about six weeks before the wedding, Bobby and I had a tremendous row. I am unable to remember what it was about. What I do recall is that in contrast to when I first met Bobby and his monosyllabic reply to every question was 'Yes', it now seemed to be 'No'.

We were on one of our inevitable walks and after being told 'No' to some of my plans for the wedding and our home, I turned to him in a rage and called him some, to me, forgettable names. Bobby still would not give in. I swept away, back towards home, expecting him to follow me. But no, he was giving me the same treatment as Mother gave me. When I realized this, I swallowed my pride and turned back. But when I reached where we had parted, he was not there. I went on to his home, but his mother said he had not come home yet, so I turned back and went to my own home, hoping to find him there. He wasn't. I waited all evening for him to call, but he didn't. I cried myself to sleep, but I was awake at five o'clock writing him notes, each of which I tore up.

I went to work looking and feeling like death, hoping he might pop into the shop in his lunch hour, but he didn't. When I arrived home in the evening after work, I was hoping to find, if not Bobby, at least a note, or even a verbal message through Mother. But there was neither Bobby nor note. Being Monday, I was expected at choir practice. If Bobby came round to the house to see me and I wasn't in, serve him right. By now, anger was beginning to replace anguish.

Singing was difficult. My throat was tight. Sebastian was not pleased with me and that upset me more. I burst into tears.

Dolores said, 'She's upset about something, Sebastian. You shouldn't go on at her tonight. Daff, come into the library.'

Dolores took me into Father Terry's library. There was a bottle of sherry on one of the bookshelves. She picked it up and searched in a cupboard for some glasses, then poured us each a glass of sherry.

'Sebastian's a bit pig-headed tonight,' she said. 'I think it's exams at school.'

'Oh, no, he's not,' I protested. 'He's marvellous. You mustn't say that about him.'

'I will if it's true. And it is,' she insisted. 'What's your problem? You don't have to tell me, of course.'

I hedged, feeling silly. 'Will Father Terry mind us having his sherry?'

'I shouldn't think so.'

There was a long pause. 'I've had a row with Bobby,' I announced.

'That's what I thought,' said Dolores.

I went on to tell her what had happened and how I wanted Bobby to get in touch with me, and I wanted to get in touch with him but wasn't sure whether to in case he was totally fed up with me and never wanted to see me again, let alone marry me.

Dolores pointed out that Bobby might be in exactly the same dilemma.

'I know. I've thought of that,' I said. 'And if I've thought of him feeling like that, why can't he think of me feeling like that and come round and see me?'

'For a start, you're not at home tonight,' Dolores said, 'and anyway, you could go on like that for ever. Someone's got to make a move and find out. What are you going to do?'

'Go round and see him. Now,' I said.

'I'll get Sebastian to give you a lift,' she said, 'after choir practice.'

So I went round to Bobby's house. Bobby welcomed me with open arms, as if nothing had happened. All his family were in bed, so it was very convenient. We sat in the Wright's front room, kissing and cuddling, me thinking 'only six weeks to go!' until about one o'clock, then Bobby walked me home. Mother came out on to the landing demanding to know where I had been and what mischief I had been up to, and muttering some nonsense about wondering whether I was entitled to wear a white wedding dress and was it worth her putting in all that effort making it?

I went to my bed feeling annoyed with Mother, Bobby and Dolores. Much as I liked and respected Dolores, I felt sure, despite the impression she had been at pains to give me, that if she and Sebastian had a row – and she had said that this did happen now and then – Sebastian would not have allowed a situation to develop in which she had to go running to him.

CHAPTER 9

The day of the wedding approached and, once Bobby and I had been reconciled after our difference, I was not assailed by doubts, fears or second thoughts, as Rita had suggested I would be, and as Dolores had hinted I might. None, that is, apart from two nights during the week before the wedding when I lay in bed feeling very fortunate and was suddenly hit by something like guilt. Perhaps I should not marry and have all this happiness, not to mention all the sexual activity about which I had fantasized? Perhaps I should sacrifice it all and become a nun? It would be an enormous sacrifice, but only enormous sacrifices were worth making, weren't they? I lay in bed, tossing and turning. Then, at about two o'clock in the morning, on the second night, the answer came to me in a flash. I could not possibly hurt Bobby in that way. He would be devastated. Such a decision could not possibly be good if it hurt someone like that. Besides, Bobby was becoming more and more interested in the church. For the last few weeks he had been reading avidly about monasteries and was fast becoming an expert on them. In fact, we had decided, because of this growing passion, to spend our honeymoon in a seaside town where there was a large Benedictine monastery.

Mother enjoyed the preparations. Her elder daughter's

wedding was an opportunity to display her skills. She threw herself heart and soul into the task. She made the cake. I was expected to admire this, and did so dutifully but otherwise took little interest and went off for another walk with Bobby. She made the dresses, my wedding dress and the bridesmaids' dresses. I stood patiently for tedious fittings, dutifully admired the dress, ignored the uneven stitching on the scalloped neckline, rose above the threat of the pearl buttons that fastened the back coming undone, and went off for another walk with Bobby. For once in my life I was making Mother happy. And it was easy. So I let her do what she wanted. I had my mind on higher things, anyway.

There was one slight negative note struck during all these preparations. Lena and Barbara were to be my bridesmaids. Lena was slim and would have no problem about looking attractive in pink satin. Barbara was plump and had quite a protruding little belly. Also, she was not the sort of girl who would look attractive in anything. Mother anticipated that whatever effort she put into the pink satin dress, Barbara was going to let her down. Mother hated Barbara. Barbara hated the fittings and my mother. Mother got impatient, complained about Barbara's plumpness, cursed a bit and stuck a pin in her. Judging by the commotion, a stranger would have thought Barbara had been stabbed at the very least. I had to calm them both down, boost Mother's morale by saying what a wonderful job she was doing, and Barbara's by saying how lovely she would look.

Bobby and I, when we were not walking between the two family homes, or deviating slightly from the route, would go over to our tiny flat and gloat over it. We had very little money, so what we did have was wisely spent on three very important items, the cooker, a carpet and the bed.

In between making dresses and cakes and generally trying to make her mark, Mother hovered around the second-hand shops and chose good quality second-hand furniture for us.

She also saw it into the flat. We had only to pay for it. Neither Bobby nor I complained about her management of our new home. I knew I would be free of her for ever very soon, and Bobby was anxious for her good-will. My mother was potentially an alarming mother-in-law. We both said how good it was of her to take such an interest. We had neither the time nor the knowledge to carry out these tasks. So we found ourselves the proud possessors of a three-piece-suite, a table and four chairs and a dressing-table and chest of drawers.

Presents began arriving. Bobby and I spent most evenings unwrapping them and recording the item and the sender on a list. Mother and Daddy gave us bed linen, including a beautiful amber-coloured bedspread. I would have preferred blue, but Mother was keen for us to have colours which were almost identical to the ones she had had when she was married. Bobby's parents were at a loss as to what to give us and in the end decided on a sum of money which we would be given on return from honeymoon.

The day before the wedding I arrived home from work to find the house packed with relatives, including Auntie Rose and Uncle Wack, Ritchie, Grandma and her sister Great-Aunt June. Where everyone was going to sleep I did not know, only that I had been given the privacy of Buster's small bedroom to myself while everyone else bedded down on mattresses, cushions or shared beds. Auntie Rose had met Bobby during several of her visits to our family and she and he liked each other. I was teased about where we were going for our honeymoon, because everyone was longing to find out and threaten to visit us there. But Bobby and I had kept it a secret.

Saying good-bye to Bobby that evening was strange and almost sad. Next time I saw him, we would be standing together at the altar, almost husband and wife. If Bobby was going to change his mind, I thought, he must tell me now.

'You scared?' I asked.

'No,' he replied. 'You?'

'No, I'm looking forward to it all.'

'It will be nice to be alone afterwards.'

'Oh, yes!' I said, so full of delicious anticipation that I swear Bobby took a short step backwards. 'Will your mum and dad be OK? Are they scared about being in a Catholic church?'

'I think they think some weird things are going to happen.'

'I'm looking forward to meeting your relatives,' I said.

'I'm looking forward to it all being over,' Bobby said with feeling, and I knew he was nervous. So was I. Neither of us must acknowledge it.

The wedding day dawned. I saw it happen because I was awake so early. The sun streamed in through the window. Lovely, I thought.

I had a bath and an early breakfast. Barbara arrived and she, Lena and I had our hair done by a neighbour. For ages, I floated around in a dressing-gown while everyone rolled up bedding, ate quick breakfasts, ironed their best clothes, and the food was laid out for the reception. As it was only a small wedding, we were having the reception at our house and Mother, with Auntie Rose's help, was doing the catering.

Then came time for me, Lena and Barbara to get dressed. Mother and Auntie Rose, in various states of dress and undress themselves, rushed in and out of our bedroom to help and advise. Everyone said we looked lovely, we said they looked lovely. Mother looked elegant in a dark green suit with a large brimmed hat and would completely overshadow Daddy.

Everything was going well until about fifteen minutes before the bride's mother and the bridesmaids were due to leave for the church. Barbara went white and announced that she had stomach-ache. She sat down heavily on the edge of the bed, her hand on the bulging little belly that had already caused problems.

'You'd better get into the bathroom,' I said as calm as anything and proud of it.

'She can't,' said Lena. 'Grandma's in there.'

Barbara sat rocking to and fro and nursing her satin-clad stomach until Grandma came out of the bathroom. Unfortunately, Auntie Rose, who was about to leave for the church with Uncle Wack, Grandma and Ritchie, came pounding up the stairs as she heard the bathroom door open.

'You can't,' shrieked Lena. 'Barbara's got a stomach-ache.'

'Oh my God!' moaned Auntie Rose, dragging on a cigarette as she stood shifting from leg to leg. 'Get in there lovey, quickly. We're supposed to be off in a minute.'

Barbara rustled into the bathroom awkwardly and closed the door. We could all hear the movement of satin and the lacquered petticoat and her little groans.

'Oh dear!' came a wail from inside the bathroom.

'What's the matter?' we all chorused, me, Lena, Mother and Auntie Rose.

'I can't find my knickers under this lot,' the anguished Barbara called back. 'Oh, it's all right.'

I went back into the bedroom for Lena to fix my veil and head-dress. I could hear Mother and Auntie Rose on the landing, Mother getting impatient, Auntie Rose trying to calm her and elicit some sympathy for Barbara.

Barbara returned looking pale and Auntie Rose almost fell into the bathroom in her desperation. At the same time there was a knock on the door and Mother shrieked.

'It's the cars. The cars. Hurry up, Rose.'

'I'm hurrying as fast as I can,' Auntie Rose called back. 'I can't hurry any more.'

Mother dashed into the bathroom as Auntie Rose came out and kissed me and Lena and Barbara good-bye, saying we all looked beautiful, especially me. Mother came out, and Barbara went in again. Mother was getting frantic, not only with Barbara, but with the weather. It was beginning to rain.

'Oh, look at it! Look at it!' she kept saying. 'What a shame! Oh, what a shame. Daffodil!'

I shrugged. 'It's only weather. Anyway, I'm getting married, not going to a beach party.'

Barbara came out and Mother checked her appearance resentfully.

'Just hold your stomach in, won't you?' she said tugging at the front hem where it was raised slightly by Barbara's fat belly. 'I should have allowed for that. Oh, why did you choose satin, Daffodil? Oh, it's time to go. It's time to go now, girls.'

She opened the door to the driver's knock and she and the bridesmaids poured out. Then they came back in again.

'What's wrong?' I asked.

'He was only telling us to be ready in five minutes' time. Oh, look, Barbara, the rain has spotted your dress!'

We spent an uneasy five minutes, not knowing what to say to each other. Daddy kept telling Mother to calm down but she just glared at him. Then the driver came up the path again. Mother opened the door before he could knock and out they poured again.

Lena looked back and laughed at me.

'Mother's in a mighty hurry to get you married,' she said, and ducked as the rain came down harder and the wind whipped her skirt and ribbons round her.

Mother clutched at her big straw hat, but too late, it lifted. Barbara rescued it from a rose bush, then had to be rescued herself when her dress caught on the thorns. How much damage was done to the dress I never knew. I was too busy getting married to investigate later.

Daddy and I were left alone with the next-door neighbour and watched from the window as Mother led the race through the rain down the garden path to the wrong car. The driver ushered her to the second car and they all got a little wetter because of her mistake.

The lull in activity gave me time to think. Was Bobby all right? Had he got to the church? Barbara had brought no message from him when she arrived and to my inquiries had just said he was 'all right'. Would Mother make it up the aisle without disgracing herself in some way? She was so anxious to make a good impression that she was doing everything wrong. Would Barbara have stomach-ache again? Would Bobby's parents be too uncomfortable in a Catholic church?

Then it was my turn. I picked up my bouquet, grinned at Daddy, who looked more nervous than I felt, and set out confidently down the garden path to the car. Once settled in the back of the car, and feeling like every bride I had ever seen, we drove sedately to the church.

As soon as we were in the porch, I began to feel really excited, not nervous or anxious, but thrilled. There was a large crowd in the church and they were all there for me and Bobby. Lena was enjoying herself and took her responsibilities as chief bridesmaid very seriously.

Father Terry was in the porch smiling reassuringly and told me that Bobby was there and quite happy. Then he left us and the activity in the church settled as Sebastian let the music he was playing trail away and paused before launching into the wedding march.

Oh, how I enjoyed walking up that aisle. There were all the members of the choir, including Dolores, and I smiled at them. Then I saw Rita and Derek, Jenny and her fiancé, and Betty, and I smiled at them. I saw, oh, such a surprise!, Wendy and her mother with the baby – I was so pleased. There were all the relatives, almost unrecognizable in their new outfits, Auntie Rose, Uncle Wack, Ritchie, Grandma, Auntie June and Buster now nearly fourteen, actually looking quite grown up. Mother was in the front pew and I knew that every time Auntie Rose looked at her she would call her 'Lady Mulligan' to herself. Across the aisle were Bobby's guests, not so many of them as on our side. His mother was dressed rather plainly and simply apart from her hat which sported an enormous long feather.

Then I was beside Bobby, who gave me a nervous smile. I grinned boldly and muttered, "You OK?" He muttered the same question back and I nodded brightly. Beside him was his cousin who was best man and whom I had not met until now.

Sebastian stopped playing when I had handed my bouquet of pink roses to Lena. The wedding service was about to begin.

It was all very solemn and Bobby and I were appropriately serious. But I had forgotten something. Father Terry began: 'Do you . . .' I froze, Father Terry could have been asking me to promise the impossible for all I had heard after that. In fact, he was. And, not hearing and not knowing did not make any difference anyway. All I was aware of was the explosion of mirth in the assembled congregation. My response, 'I do,' was delayed and Bobby and Father Terry waited anxiously . . .

Daffodil Rosemary did pull herself together and promise to take Bobby, but not without feeling the shame of having revealed her real name to the amused congregation.

Vows were exchanged, rings were exchanged, the register signed while Mother wept theatrically and the choir excelled itself. Bobby and I emerged from the church well and truly married, into a howling gale. We smiled bravely as the photographer arranged us and battled with the wind rearranging dresses, hair, my veil, Mother's hat, then we all piled thankfully into the cars to drive home for the reception.

I looked at Bobby and at my new wedding ring and felt a bit sorry for him because it was so obviously my day and, important – no vital – though he was, no one, including myself was paying much attention to him, though Bobby was not someone who ever sought the limelight. Even the reflected glow was too much for him.

The wedding reception was, as I should have anticipated, another jolly family disaster. A number of the small pearl buttons fastening the back of my dress not only came undone but fell off, and rolled about the floor. Barbara's dress came unstitched at the armhole seam and she spilt jelly down the front of it. The hem of Lena's dress came undone. Buster was sick. Auntie Rose and Uncle Wack kept making bawdy remarks about wedding nights, Mother became tense and agitated. Grandma kept calling for Mrs Wright and I wondered how she came to be on such friendly terms with my mother-in-law so quickly, before I realized she was addressing me. My new father-in-law commented loudly that the wedding cake was rather moist, while I knew that he meant downright soggy. Someone else, more sophisticated and experienced than either the Mulligans or Wrights, detected that what we were drinking was not champagne but something a lot cheaper and much less fun.

'Let's get out of here,' I muttered to Bobby.

'Yes,' he said.

'*That*,' I said emphatically, nodding towards the milling guests and their artificial jollity, 'is not what today is about.'

I could see the relief on Bobby's face. He was not the world's most extrovert husband.

In my bedroom, with the door closed, I stepped out of the wedding dress, tossed the veil aside and, in my petticoat, opened my arms wide for a cuddle. Bobby obliged. We indulged in this comforting behaviour for a few minutes while I mentally registered that now Bobby and I could do what we liked. His hands could wander where he, or I, liked, and mine could too. But they didn't, neither his nor mine.

I changed into a neat little tweed suit and felt very matronly. As we left to be driven to the station by Uncle

Wack, confetti was showered on us, and I tossed my bouquet to Lena. Unfortunately, Barbara caught it. Lena's face was like thunder.

Once round the corner, Uncle Wack briefly stopped the car so that we could shake out some of the confetti and also check for tin cans, old shoes tied on the back, and kippers stuffed up the exhaust. It was a slight disappointment to find that no one had bothered.

The confetti seemed to follow us. Wherever we stood, at Euston, in the underground, at Victoria, there it was eddying round us on the ground while we stood, embarrassed, in the middle of it, trying to pretend it was nothing to do with us.

Our hotel was something modest on the sea-front, but neither of us having stayed in a hotel before, even its modesty was intimidating. Our room had a big double bed and large windows opening out on to a balcony overlooking a still and luminous sea.

I changed into a dress in preparation for dinner, anticipating spending a romantic half hour on the balcony with Bobby, but showers of confetti fell out of my clothes and the time was spent on our hands and knees picking it up, piece by piece.

Dinner was memorable only for our self-consciousness and the speed with which we ate – or left – what was put before us. We were back in our room soon after nine o'clock.

'I'm tired,' I said, for want of something to say.

'So am I,' said Bobby. 'I think I'll get ready for bed.'

He undressed with his back to me while I undressed with my back to him. When I turned, he was standing there in all his glory wearing a pair of hideously striped pyjamas. He hardly looked at me, glamorous though I knew I was in a flowing white nightdress which, though not revealing, suggested a lot.

'Which side do you want?' I asked as we turned to face the bed.'If you don't mind,' he said, 'I've already picked that side. I've put my books on the bedside table.' So he had, I observed. There was '*Benedictine Monasteries*' and '*Marriage and Sex*,' blushingly bought a week earlier in a book shop.

Bobby looked at me briefly. 'Don't let's do it tonight,' he said.

'No,' I agreed.

'It says in the book it's not a very good time, the first night, after the ceremony and the journey and everything.'

'Yes,' I agreed, 'We've got the rest of our lives, haven't we?'

So near, yet still so far! I thought.

'And the Sung Mass at the Abbey is at eight o'clock tomorrow morning,' Bobby enthused. 'We want to be up in time for that, don't we?'

'Oh yes,' I agreed.

CHAPTER 10

Married life with Bobby ran very smoothly. For six months I was totally content, playing the little housewife, building our nest together. To add to my sense of propriety, Bobby, obsessed with monasteries ancient and modern as he was, decided that he would, in his words, 'quite like to become a Catholic'.

We were sitting round the electric fire one evening, shortly before Christmas, when he dropped what was for him, a bombshell. I was knitting at the time and nearly dropped a stitch. Actually, this piece of knitting had caused my mother some consternation as it was white and I was, due to my newly discovered talent in cooking, putting on a bit of weight. It was only an Aran-style hat for Barbara for Christmas, but Mother was not to know that.

'Would you?' I said casually, knowing that eagerness might deter Bobby. 'Why do you say that?'

'I don't know,' he replied. 'I just do.'

'I expect it was those monks you're always on about,' I said.

'I expect so.'

Pause. 'Are you going to do anything about it?'

'I don't know.' He paused this time. 'What could I do?'

'Go and have a chat with Father Terry,' I suggested.

'Another chat?'

'Oh yes. But you'll discuss different things this time.'

No reply. I knitted some ten rows. Then, from behind *The Dissolution of the Monasteries*, Bobby asked, 'How do you become a Catholic?'

'You have instruction,' I told him. 'Sister Elizabeth does it.'

'I could go when you go to choir practice,' Bobby said.

Choir practice on Monday evenings was still my regular once a week night out, my escape from domestic chores. Bobby usually stayed at home and did the washing-up on these evenings. Alas, it came to pass that, in the end, I had to do the washing-up before setting out with Bobby, me for choir practice, he for the convent to see Sister Elizabeth.

One Monday evening I came home in my usual hurry, planning to do marvellous things with the left-overs from the Sunday joint before we hurried out again. To my surprise I found Bobby in bed.

'What's the matter with you?' I demanded, not believing very much could be wrong.

'Nothing,' Bobby replied bravely. 'I think I've got flu, that's all.'

'Flu!' I stared at him. His face, peering at me blearily above the eiderdown was moist and flushed. He smelled warm and sour, an unfamiliar smell and an unpleasant one. I didn't want to go near him. I didn't want to show sympathy. I was angry.

'But it's Monday!' I said.

'Yes,' murmured Bobby from under the covers.

'Don't you want anything to eat? What about Sister Elizabeth? What about choir practice?'

'Oh, you go to choir practice. I'll be all right.'

'But I can't leave you on your own if you're ill!'

Bobby said nothing.

'Can I get you anything?' I asked dutifully.

Bobby suggested that another dose of aspirin and a drink of

hot lemon would be received with gratitude. I ministered unto his needs then sat alone at the kitchen table munching my way through doorstep sandwiches of cold lamb and pickle. When I crept into the bedroom again, Bobby was sound asleep. I found a piece of paper, wrote 'Gone to choir practice. Love, Daff', left it by his bedside table and went off to choir practice with a strange mixture of unease and elation. It was the beginning of the end.

Once Bobby had recovered from flu, the next big event in our lives was our participation in the parish retreat. A retreat is exactly what it says, an opportunity to retreat from the everyday problems of life in a place of quiet and beauty, to think about God, to pray, to discuss, to receive guidance from those qualified to give advice, and generally to take stock of one's life. Since our retreat was being held in a nearby Benedictine abbey, there was no problem about Bobby's participation. Father Terry, who was also going, said it would be an extension of Bobby's instruction. I must say I was surprised, no startled, by Bobby's enthusiasm for the occasion. I was not so happy about it. Sebastian and Dolores were also going, as were other choir members. To me, these were sophisticated, educated people. I was somewhat intimidated by them, wanted to be like them, and to be liked by them, but had no way of knowing how to do either. Beside them I felt ignorant and was sure they thought about me in the same way as I thought about me.

I knew Bobby would be even more intimidated by their status. In fact, Bobby and I had rarely been in the company of these people socially, as a married couple. I was much happier with only myself to steer through this social challenge. Steering Bobby as well was like dragging anchor. But, needing to hide my ineptitude for things social and intellectual, I agreed to go. I needed also to present myself as a happy wife, so had to support Bobby's enthusiasm.

The abbey, of course, was beautiful. Although it was cold and blustery, being late February (had the sun shone since Bobby and I married?) the gardens and grounds were bare and clear and waiting for spring, lone crocuses witnessing to the promise. Accommodation was simple, if not stark: double rooms, twin beds, log fires in the dining-room, library and lounge, vegetarian food consisting of vegetables grown by the monks, brown bread baked by the monks, and fresh milk from the abbey herds in earthenware jugs on polished wooden tables. There was something basic and earthy about it all, in contrast to the aestheticism of the abbey church and the philosophy of the Order. Bobby seemed to appreciate the same things. Not that I saw much of him, except in the dark at night across the chasm between our two beds. He seemed to spend most of the weekend in earnest conversation with various monks, or in some sort of ecstatic contemplation of the abbey church. On several occasions I glimpsed him gazing up, still and silent, at the great stained-glass windows or the soaring roof. My time was taken up with subdued but frivolous conversations in the gardens with Sebastian, or Dolores, or both, or soul-searching dialogues with Father Terry. During one of the latter, Father Terry stopped, looked at me and said.

'Are you happy, Datt?'

I went hot, cold, all temperatures in between and avoided his gaze, his sympathy.

'Yes!' I protested. 'Yes, of course I am!'

He returned his attention to the ground under his feet and started walking again. 'I just wondered, that's all. If you ever do find yourself with problems, you know where to get help, don't you?'

I felt as if I was struggling to get away, yet I was free to run in any direction I wanted.

'Yes, yes, of course,' I said.

Later that day, I recalled his words with a chilled feeling.

Sebastian and Dolores were, on behalf of a group of us in the parish, writing to the bishop. I do not recall what about, except that Sebastian and Dolores were real live-wires in the church and although I did not always understand their ideas and motives, I was always ready to support them and agree with them because I admired them, was convinced they were right and wanted to be like them. Dolores asked me if I would sign the letter, which I did readily. She laughed when I handed back the letter and pen.

'Oh dear. That's a Freudian slip,' she said.

Not being in the right frame of mind to discuss Freud with anyone, let alone Dolores, I looked at my signature. I went red – all over. I had signed myself 'Daffodil Mulligan'.

For two months I wrestled with the truth, fought it off, tried to confound it, rationalize, evade it, dodge it, anything but stare it in the face.

Then, one Wednesday afternoon, Wednesday being early closing day, I locked up the shop and, instead of going home to wash Bobby's underpants and socks, I caught a bus that went far out into the country. It was a momentary decision, made as I crossed the bus station towards home.

The bus droned along the green valley away from the town. My spirits began to lift, it seemed for the first time for months. What a beautiful day it was, late May, brilliant blue sky, trees and hedgerows frothy with white blossom. Everything sparkled. I sparkled. I was running away.

The bus dropped me in the middle of a picture-postcard village. I walked up a hill, perched on a five-barred gate and gazed hungrily over the valley. I had no idea of time, how I was going to get home, if and when there was another bus. I did not care.

When I descended from the five-barred gate, I acknowledged the truth, a terrible, shameful, exhilarating, liberating truth: I was not in love with Bobby. And I dare not confide in

Father Terry.

My life, henceforth, would revolve around Sunday morning Mass and Monday evening choir practice.

When I eventually reached home, which must have been well after seven o'clock in the evening, Bobby was immersed in *Cistercian Abbeys in Wales*, and waiting for his meal. Great helpless lump, I thought. Why couldn't he get me a meal?

He inquired, briefly, as to the reason for my late arrival home. I told him, briefly, the name of the village I had visited and set about frying some sausages. As I pricked them before dropping them into the pan, I thought, yes, Rita and Wendy had been right about sex. It was nothing.

By July, my patience was snapping. Bobby totally ignored my hostility. I was exhausted with the effort of participating in as many church activities as I could. I decided I needed a holiday and took a week off to go to Auntie Rose's alone. The day I went coincided with our first wedding anniversary. Bobby did not notice. I did not care.

Auntie Rose knew something was wrong, but I could not bring myself to explain. On returning I decided to avoid church, leave the choir and go to Mass in the next parish. Bobby was reading *The History of the Dominicans* and had a heap of washing for me to do. I did it only because he told me he needed it for a trip he had planned the following week, to some remote abbey in the North of England, alone. I was amazed to think of Bobby going all that way unaccompanied, unprompted. And I was relieved.

Meanwhile, I had stopped going to Mass, even in the next parish. Bobby had ceased his instruction with Sister Elizabeth. Dolores had written to me, asking where I was and what was wrong and Father Terry had come round to the flat, obviously with the same question, and I insisted that we did not answer the door. I had avoided my mother for nearly three months and only realized this when Lena appeared on the doorstep, joyfully announcing she had passed her three A-levels and would be going to college in September.

I could not discuss my problems with Bobby. He was such an insecure soul. I could not face the responsibility of witnessing his reaction.

There was, I concluded, only one thing to do. And I did it.

I left my job, found a room in London, packed my bags, and on the last day of September, made a quiet and unspectacular exit from my home town. After several rewrites, I had eventually written out the following for Bobby:

Dear Bobby,

I can't stand it any longer. It's not your fault. Please forgive me. I hope you get on OK. Please write to me at the address below but don't come to see me. Not yet.

Love, Daffodil

I added my new address and propped the letter on the bedside table on top of *The Future of Monastic Life*.

CHAPTER 11

So there I was, living in London, a place which my mother had always referred to as the city of sex, sin and shame. In the few excursions I had made to the capital, I had not seen much evidence of depravity. However, living in London was a different matter and my own reasons for moving there were certainly reasons of sex, sin and shame.

My worst fears were confirmed during my first evening in London, in the little room I had taken in the Hampstead area. Only in desperation would I have chosen that room, but I was desperate. It was in a large, dim Victorian house, with a tiled floor and stained-glass windows in the hall. It housed several bed-sitters and two small flats, all occupied by young women who all had their boyfriends, frequently and illegally, to stay overnight.

On my first evening I sat on my bed and stared out of the window at the houses that backed on to mine. There was nothing else to look at. The wallpaper was dingy, the view nearly as depressing to me, a country girl who had always looked out on trees and fruitful gardens and distant horizons.

From the next room a cry came, loud, long and ecstatic, reaching a peak before silence returned. I moved my gaze from the window and stared at the blank wall which separated me from my neighbour. A thrill of fear mixed with excitement went through me. I had never heard anyone making love before. In fact, until that moment, I had had no evidence that other people really did it. What Mother had implied was true – they were all at It in London, all the time. And Wendy and Rita were wrong. People did enjoy It. I was amazed, too, that the girl next door had no shame. That noise must have been heard throughout the house.

Well, I thought, as I sank into my sagging single bed, this is promising.

There were problems, of course. The next morning when I went out to explore and to find myself a job, I realized I was living directly opposite a Catholic church. At first I refused to look at it, and glared at the nuns passing me in the street. Then one day, after about two weeks, I decided that I could not go through life ignoring an institution as big and powerful as the Catholic church. The only thing to do was to have the courage of my convictions and face it. So in I walked. I sat down at the back and cried and cried. Great sobs echoed from the walls. I became aware that I was not alone – someone else was sitting across the aisle. Pulling myself together I got up and made to leave. As I passed the other figure I realized that this person was doing the same thing. Great sobs continued to echo round the walls.

Out in the sunshine, I began to laugh.

After that, my worst problem was the mouse. One night, sound asleep, I was woken by a rhythmic knocking coming from the gas cooker. Straining eyes and ears I found that it was coming from the frying pan, left on top of the cooker after use. Being on my own, I was not planning to be a slave to washing-up. I switched on the light in time to see a movement in the frying pan and brief scampering on the floor behind the cooker. Tiny footprints and lick marks had been left in the pan, which I promptly wrapped and consigned to the waste bin.

Then in the middle of the night I set about reorganizing my

cupboards and putting away all food-stuffs.

Once I had laid poison and traps, I thought I had beaten the creature, but no, another night I heard a strange rustling in my hand-bag by my bed. That evening I had had some chips on my way home and lazily left the paper in my bag. The mouse, by now starved of titbits, was licking the fat off the paper. He made several appearances after that and I soon became grudgingly fond of him. My only concern was that he would bring germs and infection that would kill me before I had started to live. Then one day I came home from work to find his poor little neck broken in my trap. I felt like a murderess. Although I cried for the mouse, I think it was Bobby I was crying for. I had treated him in rather the same way.

It was this day, on the evening of the death of the mouse, that I began to feel really concerned about Bobby. I had left three weeks ago and not heard from him. Nor from my mother to whom I had assumed he would give my new address. Apart from wondering whether Bobby had had a nervous breakdown or attempted suicide, the silence was unnerving. I had made a great statement by running away. Had it fallen on deaf ears?

Within four days of my arrival in London, after being sent by an agency hither and thither across the city for interviews, I found myself a job. It was the one at the bottom of my list, the most boring and least well paid, but they wanted me and, beginning to panic, I felt I needed them. I was to operate a switchboard for a large firm of solicitors.

Working in London was a completely different experience from working in my home town. Once I had conquered my fears of using escalators, of being suffocated in the rush-hour crush on the tube, and of having my bottom pinched, I began to enjoy travelling to work. There was nothing and no one to keep me at home, home being my room. Nor was I answerable to anyone for anything, not Mother's demands or Bobby's smelly socks.

The people I worked with were different, too. Everyone was on first-name terms and the familiarity shocked me. No one laughed when I revealed myself as Daffodil, there already being a Daphne working there. And Daffodil Mulligan, beside names like Bill Bloggs, Posy Spencer and Hildegard Blumer faded into normality.

I soon made friends, there being no other opportunity apart from my neighbour Maureen, who seemed always to be busy doing It, and the other girls in the house, who I did not dare disturb in case they were doing It, too. I didn't want it to be known that I feared loneliness, which would have been an absolute giveaway that I had no one to do It with.

Everyone at work seemed to be doing It. In fact, during my first week, when I made friends with Pat Kennedy, Bill Bloggs, Glenys Williams, Posy Spencer and Hildegard Blumer, I got information on everybody from everybody. To my innocent mind, it seemed that if they weren't actually doing It (and even doing It in the office if some of the stories were true), they were talking about It.

Lunch times were often spent in the pub, so from my first ever visit to a pub on my second day at work, I became a 'regular', sticking rigidly to bitter lemon 'because of my figure', I said, fearful to admit that I was afraid of drink. Not only Mother's lingering disapproval but the fear that alcohol might loosen my tongue held me back. I had several secrets I needed to guard, one of them being that I was not doing It.

Glenys was. She was openly living with her boyfriend, 'in sin' as Mother would have said. Hildegard, worse, was living with someone else's husband. Bill, whose name really was Bloggs but not Bill, was known to be a 'bit of a lad' and the story went that he had taken the previous telephonist down to the basement and done It, and she had left because she had changed her mind about him. During my first week there,

Glenys had a row with him because he had pinched her bottom as she came up the stairs. Actually, I think he behaved a bit improperly with me, but I was not sure and didn't want to make a fuss in case I had made a mistake. One morning, he came and stood by my swivel chair at the switchboard, and his leg was very close to mine; so close, in fact, it was touching, then pressing against mine. I moved my leg. He moved his. I swung right round on my chair and he had to step back. Pat said I should have given him the sharp end of my tongue, but I thought it might have been me being over-sensitive.

Pat, from Cork, had an attractive soft accent, a wicked sense of humour, startling blue eyes fringed with thick black lashes, and went home on the same underground line as I did. And apart from me, Pat seemed to be the only person in the whole office who was not doing It all the time. We became firm friends.

'Mulligan,' mused Pat on first hearing my name. 'That's a grand old Irish name.'

'My grandfather was,' I said.

'Where did he come from?' asked Pat, like all Irish emigrants intensely interested in their country of origin.

'I don't know. I never met him. He died before I was born and nobody has ever said much about him. He got me into the Caledonian society,' and I explained the false pretences on which I had become proficient in the eightsome reel.

'So where's your home?' was the next shrewd question. 'What are you doing in London?'

I went hot all over.

'Oh, sorry,' said Pat, 'I didn't mean to pry. It can't be as bad as the reason I'm here.'

That whetted my curiosity, and provoked some fear. What had Pat, who seemed so pleasant and open, done that could be worse than my story? 'Why are you here?' I ventured.

'Come down to the pub at lunch time and I'll tell you a bit

about myself . . .'

Pat's story appeared to be similar to my own. There had been Someone in Ireland, and it had been assumed by the families that they would both get married and live happily ever after. Having found attraction elsewhere and feeling unable to explain to anyone, Pat, like me, had fled to London when the pressure to announce the engagement suddenly became very heavy.

'I did worse than that,' I confessed, Pat's openness giving me courage. 'I'm married – I ran away.'

'Jesus, Mary and Joseph!' said Pat. 'Were you in love with Someone Else?'

I stared into my bitter lemon because I didn't want to think about that.

'Jesus, Mary and Joseph!' said Pat again.

We both sat in silence for a few minutes.

'What did your husband say?'

'I don't know. I didn't tell him. I left a note one day. I asked him to get in touch with me. But he hasn't. I'm a bit worried. I don't think I did it right. How do you end a marriage, Pat? Why hasn't he come begging me to go back?'

'Do you want him to?'

'No! But I'd like to know he's all right. It's not his fault, really,'

'He doesn't know that. When did you leave?'

'Nearly a month ago.'

'Jesus . . .' began Pat.

'I know! Anything could have happened! I suppose I'll have to go down there and see. I don't want to do that.'

'Why not?'

'I might bump into my mother,' I said.

On my way home that evening I made two resulutions – one to go to the flat to see Bobby the next Saturday, the other to write and tell Auntie Rose as much of the truth as I dared. She must have been wondering what had happened to me. I had not written to her since I had left.

I wrote to Auntie Rose that evening. In fact I wrote to her several times and it was well past midnight when I had produced the definitive version. At that time I was extremely pleased with it, so pleased, in fact, that I copied it out. It was truly a masterpiece. It said everything, explained everything and was totally honest.

I put both the letter and the copy in my handbag and pondered the problem on the way to the tube station. The first letter-box I walked by, but I happened to be at the second one when I was chiding myself about pussy-footing and protecting people who loved me. I shoved the letter in the box. By the time I reached the tube station, I was wishing I hadn't, but by the time I reached work I had convinced myself that I had done the right thing.

Naturally, I was somewhat preoccupied and Glenys, Pat and Bill asked me several times what was wrong. After work, Pat suggested that the pair of us take a trip down to the pub.

'Bitter lemon?'

'No thanks,' I said. 'Brandy and ginger.'

'Jesus, Mary and Joseph! You're in a state.'

I had decided that with the help of a small drop of alcohol, I might be able to confide in Pat about what was bothering me, despite the fact that it was confiding in someone that *was* bothering me. But Pat, craftily talking about everything else while I was sipping my first drink, forced me to have another. Then came the question.

'So what's the matter with you today, Daffodil?'

'I thought you'd never ask!' I laughed with relief. 'For a start, I've got to go down to see my husband on Friday evening.'

'Are you staying the night?' Pat asked incredulously.

'Goodness, no!'

'Then why are you going Friday evening?'

'Because I don't really want to do it – I want to get it over with and have the weekend to myself. Also, there are people down there I don't want to meet, and I'm not likely to meet them on a dark Friday evening. I'm more likely to see these people in daylight on a Saturday.'

'Who?'

Silence.

'Ah, you can trust me. I've got a skeleton in the cupboard too, remember.'

'Yours isn't as bad as mine!'

'Sorry. I didn't know we were competing.'

'Look,' I said, beginning to feel careless of my behaviour, 'the whole problem is, I've already told one person and it's worrying me.'

'Jesus, Mary and Joseph! You mean you've got this enormous secret on your conscience and you've only told one person? No wonder you're in a state!'

Silently I took out the copy of my letter to Auntie Rose and passed it across the table. I went to buy another drink for each of us. The barman seemed far away. I didn't care.

When I sat down, Pat had nearly finished the letter and was laughing. I was mortified.

'What are you laughing at?' I demanded, hoping fervently that Auntie Rose too would see the funny side of the letter. She was always so keen to see the funny side.

Pat took another drink before replying.

'You won't believe this . . . In fact, I can't believe it . . . I would never have guessed!'

'What?' I said, pounding my fist on the table and jumping up and down.

Pat spluttered. 'Such a coincidence. A miracle. You'll never guess! I just can't believe it! It's the same with me! Do you understand?' I stared. 'My story's the same!'

I continued to stare. Was I being mocked, taken for a ride?

Was this some trick? Had I fallen foul of one of the dark goings-on in London. 'You can't – you can't mean it?' I gasped.

'Mean it! I've never been more serious!' Pat's laughter belied the words.

I began to grin. 'What luck!' I said, relaxing.

Then we both roared with laughter. Tears of mirth ran down my cheeks. I rolled about in my chair. People looked at us. We hugged each other.

Needless to say, Pat had to see me home that evening. I would have been a menace on the escalator alone.

'Look,' said Pat, when we sat in my room drinking coffee, 'why don't you postpone your trip to hubby on Friday night, and come with me. I belong to a group, it's a support group, and I guess support is something you could do with, right now. There's a meeting on Friday evening, at a member's house. We just sit around and talk, mostly. It'd do you good.'

I thought for a moment. I could easily go to see Bobby on Saturday evening. 'OK,' I said.

So on Friday evening I went to meet Pat's group of friends for the first time. There I met Chris.

It was lust at first sight.

CHAPTER 12

The meeting was held in a cramped flat in Shepherd's Bush, in a smoke-filled living-room. There were about a dozen men and women there, mostly between twenty and thirty-five years old, I estimated. I felt very nervous, very gauche and was sure everyone thought I was a complete idiot. Pat offered me a cigarette, which I accepted in a vain attempt to appear cool, calm and collected. I went giddy when I dragged on it and had to remove myself from my perch on the arm of a chair and sit on the floor.

'I'm shy,' I said to Pat in a whisper.

'Nonsense! So am I,' was the confusing response.

Then Chris came in

Now most young women of my age were dreaming of tall, dark, handsome men, possibly rich, certainly solvent.

Not me. Not once I had seen Chris. Chris was broad and fair and, I soon learned, unemployed. Not attractive in the conventional sense of good looks, but exuding an indefinable charm, even magnetism; perhaps power was the word. I don't know, except that I was fascinated and frightened.

Chris sat down near me. And smiled at me.

'Hallo! Who are you?'

'I'm fine, thank you,' I said.

Chris laughed. 'I said *who* are you? Not, *how* are you?

What's your name? You know . . ..'

I went red. 'Oh, sorry. My name is Daffodil Mulligan.'

'Hallo Daffodil. I'm Chris Smith. You're new in this lot, aren't you?'

'Yes. I came with Pat,' I said.

'Oh, you came with Pat!' Chris and Pat exchanged grins. I felt excluded. 'You nervous?' Chris asked in a much softer voice.

'Terrified!' I whispered.

'Don't be. We're all a nice crowd. And we were all nervous the first time we came to a meeting.'

I was overwhelmed. I don't know what by, but I was overwhelmed. It could have been relief, Chris's kindness, or something else. I strongly suspect it was something else.

Later I managed to ask Pat, 'Who is Chris?'

'Jesus, Mary and Joseph!' came the predictable exclamation, 'You're not falling for Chris, are you?'

'Certainly not!' I protested.

I went to see Bobby on Saturday afternoon. I figured that as it got dark early, if I arrived at about six o'clock I would have an hour in which to explain to Bobby before setting out for London again.

I left my new home and travelled to the main-line station feeling very anxious about the sort of reception that was ahead of me. There had been no word from Bobby, nor from anyone else in the family. I wondered if he was trying to keep my leaving a secret in the hope that I would return and our lives would go on the same as before. I had been so preoccupied with trying to sort myself out, both emotionally and practically, that I had not had time to spare for wondering too deeply about Bobby.

Or Mother.

My stomach did several somersaults. I vowed to shelve her for a week, if not longer.

I boarded the train and whom should I see, sitting in the same compartment, quite obviously returning home from Christmas shopping in the West End, but Sebastian and Dolores . . .

I froze, then stumbled out again, found another compartment and sat back, trying to relax. Doors slammed, the whistle blew, footsteps clattered outside and a late passenger lurched in as the train moved forward. She sat down a few seats further up the compartment. I met her eyes.

'Oh, my God!' I said.

'Oh, my God!' she said.

It was Lena.

We stared at each other for ages, then she gathered her belongings and moved nearer to me.

I was at a loss for words. It appeared that Lena was too.

'How are you?' she said.

'I'm fine,' I replied. 'How are you?'

'I'm fine,' she said.

There was a long pause.

'How's Bobby?' she asked.

'Oh, Bobby . . . he's fine,' I said. I couldn't believe it. Didn't she know? 'How's college?'

'Oh, fine, fine,' she said.

'Are you enjoying it?'

'Oh yes, yes.'

'Are you home for the weekend?'

'Oh, yes. Yes. I'm home for the weekend. What about you?'

'What do you mean?' I asked cagily.

She seemed to gather herself together. 'What about you? Been to London?'

'Yes,' I said truthfully. This was some conversation!

'Christmas shopping?'

I had a very strong feeling that Lena had several advantages over me. This was a very unfair confrontation.

'Well, no.' I spread my hands out, for I had no parcels. She was waiting for my explanation. Does she know? 'I went to book some theatre tickets.'

The train jerked and swayed, gathering speed. I was thrown against the people on either side of me. I felt visible and vulnerable and knew they were all listening to our conversation. Lena and I leaned across towards each other, trying to meet each other's gaze brazenly.

'Oh, I see. It's ages since I've seen you. Must have been before the beginning of term. What have you been doing with yourself?'

'Oh, nothing much,' I lied 'Same boring old things. Housework, shopwork, housework, shopwork.'

'Really?' she smiled. 'Does nothing exciting ever happen to you, Daff? Have you settled down at last, learned to be a good little girl and stop being a problem to everybody?'

Right now, she was being a problem to me. I wanted to disappear, or cry. I didn't know which to choose. I was stuck on the train for the entire forty-five-minute journey.

I remained silent.

'No kiddywinks on the way yet?' Lena went on.

'You'd be surprised,' I said.

'So would you!' she retorted. She knows, I thought. But how? I began to feel sick, it was my only escape. I stood up.

'Excuse me,' I said, moving towards the toilet.

'Where are you going?' she said.

'Toilet. Afternoon sickness,' I mumbled and left her.

After that I avoided her, and even when I caught a glimpse of her as I left the station I turned the other way

I felt very strange being in the town where I had lived for twenty years and had left for ever a few weeks earlier. I tried to slink along the roads, avoiding Lena, Sebastian and Dolores and anyone else whom I might know and who might ask awkward questions.

The flat was in darkness. I knocked first anyway, just in

case Bobby was asleep or listening to the radio in the dark to save electricity. When there was no answer, I let myself in with my key.

The place smelled damp and cold. I picked up a mountain of post from the doormat, then darted from room to room switching on lights. Everything was very orderly, just as I had left it, in fact. Even the letter I had left for Bobby on the bedside table, was still propped up on *The Future of Monastic Life*.

Truth dawned. Bobby did not even know I had left him.

But where was he?

I sat on the bed and sifted through the post. There were two letters from Lena from college, there were bills, there were red notices because the bills hadn't been paid, there were three hand-scribbled notes from Mother, one hand-delivered letter from Father Terry and a note and a hand-delivered letter from Dolores. And one in Bobby's handwriting addressed to me.

I read Mother's first.

Monday evening
Dear Daffodil and Bobby,

I've been round to see you twice this week and you've been out on both occasions. Do you want to come to tea for my birthday on Sunday week?

Love, Mother and Daddy

Monday 7th November
Dear Daffodil and Bobby,

Where were you yesterday? We haven't heard from you for nearly three weeks and you're not in tonight. Is everything all right?

Love, Mother and Daddy

Tuesday evening 8th November

Dear Daffodil,

I went to your shop today and they said you had *left*. I rang Bobby's work number and they said he had left. Where are you both?

Love, Mother

Then I read Father Terry's:

Dear Daffodil and Bobby,

No answer when I called. Everyone concerned because no one has seen you for three weeks.

Can we help?

God Bless, Fr Terry

The note from Dolores read:

Dear Daffodil,

What's up? Please get in touch. You've suddenly vanished off the face of the earth.

Love, Dolores

Then I opened Bobby's letter. It was dated three days after I had left.

Dear Daffodil,

I'm sorry. I can't stand it any longer. I didn't realize when we got married that I wasn't cut out for it. I'm going to find out if you can be a monk if you've been married. I'll be staying near one of my favourite monasteries and see if I can worm my way inside soon. I'll write again when I'm settled.

Love, Bobby

I sat still for a brief moment, then gathered all the letters and bills and stuffed them into my handbag. My one aim was to get back to London and talk things over with Pat.

There was a ring on the doorbell. Not thinking, I answered it.

On the threshold, seething with anger and hell-bent on retribution, was Mother.

I had never seen Mother walking so tall. She swept past me without waiting for me to ask her in. She stood glowering and towering above me. I had often been afraid of her, but never so afraid as now. I hesitated by the open door and reasoned rapidly that I had three choices: I could close the door, thereby indicating to Mother that she was welcome, I could leave it open, indicating that she was not, or I could flee through it. A fourth option, that of getting hold of Mother and shoving her out of the flat was, of course, out of the question.

I left the door open

Mother sailed into our living-room and sat down on one of the dining chairs she had so kindly chosen for us.

'So, you've come back!' she said.

'No,' I said.

'No?' she almost shrieked. 'You are a bad wicked girl. This is the end. I've just about had enough of you. All your life you've been a problem to me. I never thought it would come to this. What have you got to say for yourself?'

I observed that Mother, since I had left, had finally achieved her ambition of owning a fur coat – actually, it was fake-fur, but she wore it with real pride.

'Not much,' I said.

'To think I should raise a monster like you. I am ashamed. Ashamed!'

'Why, what's any of it got to do with you?'

'What's it got to do with me? After all I've done for you?'

Mother leaned back in the chair. She seemed to be settling in for a long argument, and an argument that she would win, too.

'Look, Mother, I'm a big girl now. Whatever I've done, whatever I am, is not your responsibility. It's mine. And I'll deal with it. Now, thank you for your concern, but I'll live my life the way I feel best.'

I was shaking. Memories of the gate to the education office flashed into my mind.

'Where did I go wrong?' wailed Mother, trying a different approach.

'You didn't. You've done a wonderful job. You just slipped up a bit with Lena, that's all.' That startled her.

'What do you mean?'

'I mean she's a bit catty. I didn't think much of the way she behaved towards me on the train.'

'Train? What train?'

I moved impatiently. 'The train we came down on. The London train, this afternoon.'

'Lena came on the coach from Cheltenham.'

I paused. Something didn't quite make sense. 'Then how did you know I was here?'

'Lena told me. She said she saw you at the bus station.'

Bus station? I thought, confused. 'That's right,' I said, slowly, my mind working away. So I was not the only one with secrets. 'Now would you mind leaving? I'll come and see you another time. Right now I want to get back to London.'

'Get back?'

'Yes, I'm going back. Tonight.'

'You've not come back to Bobby?'

Impatience and confusion made me stamp my foot. 'Bobby's left me.'

I expected some of the sympathy that Mother was trying to elicit from me. I did not receive it.

'Left you? I'm not surprised. It was probably your insatiable demands that drove him away.'

'What do you mean?'

Mother's hand went up to her face. 'You know what I mean,' she said turning away. The explanation was emitted with something like a hiccup. 'Sex!'

There was a silence.

'Oh!' I said after a while, feeling daring. 'You mean sex.'

'That's right! Sex! Sex! Sex!' she spat the word three times. 'That's all you ever think about.'

'You mean there are other things?'

She took me seriously. 'Of course there are!' she blazed.

I shook my head. 'Yes, you did slip up a bit, now I come to think of it. You didn't tell me that, you know. I do hope Lena isn't under the same impression.'

'Daffodil, stop being clever. You've got hard. You've changed.'

She meant I'd got worse, more of a problem to her now.

It was tiring, standing for this conversation, and I was on edge because the front door was still open. But sitting down or closing the door would have given Mother permission to prolong her visit.

'Oh, I've changed all right,' I agreed.

Mother sighed dramatically. 'That poor boy!'

'Which one?' I asked.

'Bobby, of course. Though knowing what I now know, I wouldn't be surprised if there were a dozen others.'

'Hey, be careful what you're saying. Bobby is perfectly all right. *He* left *me*, you know.'

'That is not what I heard.'

'What did you hear? Who's been talking?'

'Your dear Auntie Rose. *My* sister.'

Well, it looked like Auntie Rose, my oldest and truest friend, had let me down. She must have been shocked by the contents of my letter. Perhaps she felt I had let *her* down. For once, Auntie Rose had been unable to see the funny side. I was stunned. There was nothing to say.

Having established that she now had her sister totally on

her side and against me, Mother then swept out in her new fake-fur coat which I had been remiss enough to fail to admire.

I gathered my belongings together, switched off all the lights and left in nearly as much of a hurry as Mother had My one desperate aim was to get back to London and to pour out my troubles to Pat, the only friend I had left in the world.

CHAPTER 13

As I trudged to and from the tube station during the next week, I brooded about Auntie Rose. My one visible means of support she had always been, and now I felt betrayed by her. As I sat glumly on the tube train with thousands of other commuters, who by the look of them all had problems with Auntie Rose, I mentally wrote many a letter.

'Dear Auntie Rose,' I rehearsed on Monday, 'I don't want to upset you, but, do you realize what you've done to me? It's not that I mind Mother knowing, it's just that I trusted you so much that I didn't think I had to ask you not to tell her.'

Or on Tuesday: 'Dear Auntie Rose, what Mother always said about you is true. I wish you joy of one another. You will never see me again.'

By Friday, I had refined it to, 'Dear Auntie Rose, How could you? Why did you do it? I can't go on – Mother hates me, you hate me . . .'

And I envisaged the reply. 'Dear Daffodil, Pull yourself together. It's not the end of the world. Why hadn't you told your mother? And what about your poor father in all of this?'

Yes, there was Daddy. He would be worried about me. I would have loved to go and see him but the price was seeing Mother. She guarded Daddy from the excesses of Daffodil like a dragon guarded a fairy princess.

And what was Lena up to?

And money. That was another problem. Since I had been in London I had been spending all my earnings on myself. The food in London's cosmopolitan shops was so exciting. And I was putting on weight again, so needed new clothes. And here I was, with electricity bill, water rates, hire purchase, rent probably not paid either, all in Bobby's name, and none of Bobby's money coming in. Meanwhile he was living it up, I supposed, in some self-sufficient monastery feeding on free-range eggs, home-produced milk and honey and vegetables straight out of a well and naturally fertilized garden.

My life's search had not ended with marriage. I was now feeling that it had not even begun.

Furthermore, Christmas was around the corner. The probability was that I would be spending it on my own.

Problems demanded action, even mistaken action. Just sitting and waiting did not help.

So I wrote to Bobby's parents. Pat said to pray about the rest of the problems and what about us spending Christmas together?

On Friday Pat and I went to the meeting again. There were mostly the same faces there as the previous week, apart from two who were not familiar and did not make an impression on me. That is, not much of a positive impression. One of them was called Chloë. I took an instant dislike to her, mostly because she seemed so enviably comfortable and at ease for someone attending for the first time. Even on my second visit I was nervous and shy. And I was waiting for Chris to make a grant entrance again.

Grand it was, too, if that's the word to describe someone bursting through the door, wearing tight jeans and T-shirt, eating chips from paper and shouting 'Hi!'

Chris made straight for me and sat down beside me even

though there was no other room. I was immensely pleased, as well as overwhelmed again.

'How are you?' Chris asked me, offering me a chip which I didn't want but accepted.

'Oh, OK, thanks,' I said. 'And you.'

'Fine! Fine!' and called out, 'Hi, how are you?' to Chloë.

For a brief instant I discovered what real, searing jealousy was.

'A friend of a friend' said Chris to me by way of explanation. 'She's got a lot to say for herself, I don't like that sort.'

I relaxed thankfully. Real, searing jealousy was not comfortable. Anyway, it was against my principles.

Chris talked about this, and that, and the car, which was a Sunbeam Rapier. 'I've looked after her well. And that's difficult on the dole, you know. I try to do any work on her myself. It's cheaper that way, but I suppose it's just as well I haven't got a job, I wouldn't have time to work on her if I did. Just put the anti-freeze in. I'll give her a good spin tomorrow. D'you drive?'

'No,' I said. 'I've never had the time and the money, nor the interest really.'

'What d'you do at weekends, then?' Obviously Chris could not imagine what people did in their spare time if they had no car.

'Oh, lots of things. I see Pat sometimes. Go for walks, finding my way round London. Last week I went to see my husband. I'm going down again tomorrow.'

'You're married?'

'Well, yes, and no!' I laughed lightly. 'I left my husband. Last week, I found out that he'd left me, too. On the same day, I think. If we can never establish who left who first, we'll have to treat it the way courts do when husband and wife die at exactly the same moment – take it that the eldest left first, that's him.'

Chris seemed very interested in my sordid little story. 'How will you get there?'

'Tube, train and walk. It's not bad, really.'

'I could take you if you like. Give the car a spin. And save you some trouble.'

My heart fairly bounced inside my chest. I was sure Chris could see it.

'That's kind of you,' I said, breathlessly. 'Thanks very much.'

'That's OK. Now, tell me about your husband.'

I knew nothing about cars but was given to understand that Chris's car was something to be admired. So, when it was parked outside the house on Saturday morning, I admired it – generally, of course, for I had no idea of its specific attributes. What I did learn was that it was nicknamed the 'Passion Wagon'.

I soon found out that speed was of paramount importance. I was terrified, especially as we sped up the motorway at an illegal 85 mph. My eyes were fixed on the spot ahead where another vehicle would be if we were to crash into it. I was even more terrified when Chris, eyes off the road ahead, turned to glance at me fondly – yes, fondly – and said, 'Enjoying yourself?'

'Oh, yes,' I gulped, hardly registering the fondness. 'But I don't like going fast.'

'Beautiful, isn't she?' Chris grinned, slipping down to a mere 70 mph. The motorway continued to flash past.

By the time we arrived at the flat, my only concern was my immediate survival. Any fears of meeting people I knew were slight by comparison.

There were only a few letters, none from Bobby, and a bill waiting on the doormat for me. I decided to remove my note to Bobby from the bedside table and also return *The Future of Monastic Life* to the library. Since I had the – doubtful –

advantage of Chris's car I also packed a few items such as sheets and towels, of which I had initially taken the absolute minimum. I did not expect Bobby, when I eventually tracked him down, to want double sheets.

Chris offered to go into the library with the book in case I met anyone, so we parked nearby. I was about to say that I hoped no one would recognize me sitting in the car, when who should I see but Mother.

'Oh my God!' I gasped.

'What?' said Chris.

'Mother,' I said.

'Whose?' said Chris.

'Mine!' I said, ducking.

'Where?' said Chris.

'There!' I said pointing to the fake-fur approaching not five yards away.

'Here. Put these on,' said Chris, reaching into the glove compartment and shoving a large pair of sunglasses at me.

I obeyed. Chris was gone. Mother stopped, not two yards away. But she was not looking at me. I turned my head. Approaching Mother from behind me were Bobby's mother and Barbara.

I was wearing a scarf round my neck. I pulled it over my head and wound down the window a little.

'Good morning Mrs Mulligan,' said Mrs Wright, cowering.

Mother put on her best sympathetic air. She was, I could see, going to be noble about her part in this and disown me completely.

'Good morning, Mrs Wright. How is poor Bobby?'

Poor Bobby, I thought. Why does he get all the sympathy?

Mrs Wright was amazed. 'Bobby is all right, Mrs Mulligan thank you. We had a postcard from him last week.'

'A postcard?' It was Mother's turn to be amazed. 'He's been away, then?'

Mrs Wright was amazed again. She took a step back. 'Oh, yes. It was too much for him. I'm ever so sorry about Daffodil.'

Mother looked cross. 'I'm sorry your son ever got mixed up with her.' Listening had never been one of Mother's most notable skills.

Mrs Wright took another step backwards at this apparent sudden change from sympathy to hostility. 'Yes. Come on, Barbara.'

'You're keeping well?' Mother asked, too late, smiling like a barracuda.

'Yes, thank you,' said Mrs Wright and hurried past her pushing Barbara ahead of her. She would not, in any case, have inquired after Mother's health, not if she had any sense. Mother would have told her. In detail.

When Chris came back I was curled up with merriment.

'My mother doesn't know my mother-in-law doesn't know and my mother-in-law doesn't know my mother doesn't know.' I burbled. 'Serves Mother right. She should have listened to me last week.'

'Reckon. I'd better get you out of this town,' said Chris. 'Seems you can't move without seeing someone you know.'

We spent the rest of the day mooching around another nearby, bigger town, having a quick bite to eat in a Wimpey Bar.

We drove back to London in the late afternoon, me praying all the way. I wondered, with a thrill of excitement, what Chris had planned for the evening.

I never found out.

As I stepped out of the car, a voice from the doorway called out to me: 'Daffodil!'

I knew the voice.

'Auntie Rose!' I shouted and she emerged from the shadows.

'Daffodil, love, I've been waiting all day! Are you all

right?'

And we fell into each other's arms.

Chris mumbled something about 'See you!' and drove off, to my horror and disappointment. I took Auntie Rose up to my room.

'I didn't know she didn't know!' Auntie Rose protested for the umpteenth time, even though I had forgiven her when she explained the first time.

Auntie Rose, ever anxious to help, or to put Lady Mulligan, as she called Mother, in her place, wrote to her saying, in so many words, 'Poor Daffodil, why didn't you tell me, I could have helped her, she could have come here, what shall we do?' She also wrote to Lena, in the same vein.

Mother, ever anxious to score over her sister, wrote back and said 'It's none of your business. Daffodil has always been a problem. She must sort herself out. She never considers anyone else. She'll be back soon.'

Auntie Rose, thinking I must be suffering all on my own in some squalid basement in the worst part of that city of sex, sin and more sin, came rushing to my aid.

But I was out. And, how wonderful, Hampstead was quite pleasant. She had had all day to find out, wandering around, waiting for my return.

'But I can't go back!' I had explained to Auntie Rose. 'Even if I wanted to. Bobby's run off to a monastery. Mother wouldn't listen. *She* doesn't know *that*.'

We talked all evening, except for when we made a brief dash round the corner to the fish and chip shop. Auntie Rose didn't understand everything, and said so, but she didn't expect to understand. I tried to explain but it didn't matter that I couldn't.

Then, as Auntie Rose sat drinking yet another cup of my cheap instant coffee, while we recapped on the state of play of family politics, I heard the beginnings of a now familiar sound.

It came from Maureen's room and started softly, rising in a slow but graduating pitch. I wondered if I could camouflage the sound and stopped wondering when Auntie Rose's face registered recognition.

'My God!' said Auntie Rose, nearly as embarrassed as I was. 'She's enjoying herself!'

'That's Maureen,' I said, unnecessarily.

'Obviously not alone,' said Auntie Rose, which observation brought a whole new set of questions to my mind.

Auntie Rose had planned to return home the next day, so I pulled the bed apart and shared out the blankets. Auntie Rose had the mattress on the floor. I had the divan base. It was a bit hard. But I would not have slept anyway: I was too fidgety about Chris.

Auntie Rose left the next day, pressing the equivalent of a month's rent for my room in my hand and urging me to go down to see her at Christmas. I knew I wouldn't now because I had agreed to be with Pat, but it was lovely to have the invitation.

I had a lot of news to tell Pat at lunch time on Monday and some advice to ask.

'I had thought Chris was interested in me.' I confessed, 'until the confusion at the front door on Saturday evening. Auntie Rose appeared and Chris just sort of vanished.'

'Perhaps you've got it wrong and Chris isn't at all interested in you,' Pat suggested.

'Then why go to all the trouble of taking me down to the flat on Saturday?'

'Kindness. Chris is like that.'

I began to wonder if Pat was teasing. I was certain with the next comment. 'I thought you weren't interested in Chris, anyway. That's what you told me last week.'

'I'm not really. It's just that I suspect that that wretched Chloë Whatnot has got her eyes on Chris and she wouldn't be good for *anyone*, let alone Chris.'

'Bidgood.'

'What?'

'Bidgood. Chloë Bidgood,' said Pat.

'What a name! By the way, I've actually got some news about Bobby at last. I had a letter from his parents. They've given me an address to write to. They say he's perfectly all right. He's making plans but is afraid to get in touch with me, in case he's upset me.'

According to my mother-in-law, Bobby was alive and well and living in a convent in Kent. Yes, a convent, working as a gardener.

CHAPTER 14

The week passed slowly because I was looking forward to Friday, and to the meeting. But when Pat and I arrived, there was no Chris. Chloë Bidgood was there, though, flaunting her long legs and laughing loudly. Distasteful though it was, I spoke to her. I asked her how she knew of the existence of the group.

'Oh, Chris told me,' she said.

I remarked upon the absence of the person in question, very casually, of course.

'Oh, Chris doesn't usually come here,' she said. 'This isn't really Chris's cup of tea at all.' She paused and added quietly, almost sympathetically, 'I wouldn't have thought you were, either.'

I was furious. How I hated her! My Mother was right about Londoners. Chloë was unashamedly cockney, a cockney with style, but cockney all the same. I went home, thoroughly depressed. Here was I, on the brink of falling in love with Chris, who plainly wasn't interested, while my husband enjoyed himself in a convent.

The next day I had an agonizing back-ache and stayed in bed. At about half-past eleven my bell rang, jerking me out of my doze. I pulled on my dressing-gown, stabbed my feet into my shabby slippers, and staggered downstairs, catching sight of my tousle-haired reflection in the mirror.

I hoped it was nobody important. I expected it to be Pat.

It was Chris.

'Aren't you going to ask me in?' asked Chris, grinning.

'Why, yes,' I said, opening the door wide. 'I was just surprised to see you.'

'I thought you might be,' said Chris.

I led the way upstairs to my room and shut the door.

'I'm sorry it's such a mess,' I said weakly. 'I was asleep.'

'Got any coffee?'

'Er, yes. I'll make some. Do sit down.'

Why is it that the moments one dreams of are always spoiled by the setting? The room was untidy, my clothes strewn everywhere, mostly on the floor. The bedclothes were thrown back, like a sleezy and unsubtle invitation. I had on a dressing-gown that had a visible history of eating breakfasts and suppers in bed. And, worst of all, yesterday's knickers were lying on the floor, next to the chest of drawers. The room was stuffy, smelling of sleep, sweat and God knows what else.

What should I do first? Make a grab for the knickers or the kettle?

I put the kettle on.

'How was your aunt? asked Chris.

'Oh, fine, fine.' The gas wouldn't light. 'She was fine. We had a long talk. She understands everything. She doesn't think I'm bad, or anything. She was a great help.' I burbled on to hide my embarrassment and other feelings. Casually, I removed the under-garments decorating the room, folded them away neatly, straightened the bedclothes and opened the window.

'I thought it best that I disappeared,' Chris explained. 'I wanted to come and see you last Sunday.'

Then why the hell didn't you? I asked silently, pouring cups of coffee in a sloppy manner that matched the room and my appearance. I made no reply. There was a long pause.

'Aren't you going to ask why I didn't come to see you on Sunday?'

'Because my aunt was here? Sugar?'

'Thanks. No. I didn't know your aunt was still here then.'

I sat down on the edge of my bed. I risked looking Chris in the eye, but only briefly. I was being forced to ask the question required of me.

'Why did you want to come to see me on Sunday.'

At that moment I was aware of the beginning of the cry of the lesser-copulating Maureen next door. Chris recognized the sound and gave it total attention. As soon as the noise stopped, Chris, putting coffee cup aside, clapped and cheered loudly.

'Shh!' I said, embarrassed.

Chris laughed. 'Where were we? Oh yes, I was trying to explain why I wanted to see you on Sunday. Yes. I wanted to ask you, to tell you that I'd like you to be my girl.'

Oh – what a delicious moment!

'Oh!' I said cheekily, with a sidelong glance (pure instinct! I swear I hadn't learned it anywhere). 'So why didn't you? Have you changed your mind?' A picture of Chloë Bidgood, long legs, loud laugh, came into my mind.

'I thought I wasn't good enough for you,' Chris said.

I remember that day. It was the Saturday two weeks before Christmas. I celebrate it mentally every year, as the anniversary of the day I . . . what? grew up? arrived? found out? The day that I did It - properly, that is - the day I enjoyed It, found out what It was really like, had my dreams, ideals confirmed. And it was not only every bit as beautiful, as ecstatic as I had imagined it would be, it was better.

Chris and I made love that day. I felt very daring, but only for a while. I felt naughty, a little bit guilty too; even if my husband had left me I was still being unfaithful. But when you have been as good as I had been all through my life, actually to break a rule is not just liberating, it is positively creative.

So I found out at last.

Having found out, I was left with a new problem. It was not enough. It was wonderful, but It was not enough.

I suppose it is always progress to find out what you don't know.

'Here we are,' Pat said in the pub at lunch time one day the following week, 'staring in the mouth of Christmas, and me not having done one thing about it. I'll send me mother a cheque.'

As far as Pat was concerned, that was Christmas dealt with. I was far more conscientious. Anxious that Mother should have some benefit from her run-away daughter living in London, I spent every penny I could spare on luxurious items for the family – liqueurs, expensive chocolates from Harrods, glacé fruits, succulent fresh fruits and nuts that I knew they had never tasted. All this I placed in a box elaborately decorated with coloured paper and tinsel and set off, grimly, one evening, a few days before Christmas, to do my duty and confront them all with my reality. My relationship with Chris had given me a new confidence. I could now face an evening of haranguing.

Mother greeted me on the doorstep with a sniff and stepped back reluctantly to let me in. Daddy welcomed me warmly as though he had seen me yesterday and nothing had changed. That made Mother angry. She was reluctant to leave me alone with him in case he said something nice to me. Daughters who let down their parents do not deserve anything nice to be said to them.

Buster, who was now sixteen, pimply and brainwashed by Mother's opinions of me, stood in a corner surveying me hostilely until Mother asked him to go and make some tea. He crawled away as though she had, by the request, done something awful to his manhood.

'You shouldn't have bothered about tea,' I said brightly, bringing a bottle of sherry from my bag. 'We could have this. Have you got some glasses?'

Mother curled her lip. 'Drink!' she said with a quiet contempt that diagnosed, in one word, my utter depravity and loss to civilization.

I tried again and presented them with my carefully decorated box. Mother ignored it, although I could see that far from pleasing her, my gesture had only made her angry. So I concentrated on Daddy, showing him the contents one by one and he responded with interest and pleasure.

Buster came in with the tea.

'Where's Lena?' I asked suddenly.

'She's still at college,' Mother said. 'She's working *very* hard.'

'She must be,' I said, recalling clearly that in her last superficial but newsy letter, she had written that her end of term was some ten days before Christmas. What was Lena up to? The fact that Mother didn't know surely indicated only one thing – sex!

Buster was detailed to walk me to the railway station as it was late when I left. He didn't say much, except, 'Mother said you'd be back home by Christmas.'

'Back *here*, you mean? She's wrong, then, isn't she?' I was cross. No one had asked me what I was doing for Christmas. For all they knew, I could have been on my own.

Christmas with Pat was great fun. We went to Midnight Mass together and we both cried all the way through. Carols recalled previous Christmasses, in the bosom of my fond family when I, in my innocence then, had been able to make the judgement that Christmas with them was a waste of time and charity. How I would have loved my exile to be lifted and to be back there, quarrelling, arguing, complaining in the way only a family can.

The fun was overshadowed by one problem. Because it was Christmas we shelved discussion until the end of the day, by which time we were both exhausted with laughter, food and wine. I had had a long telephone call from Chris, holed up dutifully with ageing parents in Kent, but who promised to dash back to London to see me the day after Boxing Day. I did not confide in Chris about the unnerving brief note I had received from Bobby on the morning of Christmas Eve.

'Dear Daff,' wrote Bobby on a scrap of paper folded into a Christmas card showing the inevitable picture of an abbey.

> Here is some money towards the rent. Must see you as soon as possible. It's urgent. Can you get down here? I have no more money.
>
> Love, Bobby

Pat quizzed me as we picked at the chicken carcass on the evening of Christmas Day. 'What do you think he wants?'

'I am terrified,' I said slowly, 'that he's going to ask me to go back. Have some stuffing.'

'And you don't want to? Got any pickle?'

'No! I'm happy here. I've got Chris. I like my job.'

'You don't have to, then.'

'No. But it was so nice and comfortable us both wanting to leave each other. He'd have no job to go back to. There's no end owing on the rent,' I licked my fingers. 'I'd feel sorry for him if I didn't, if he asked me. And would it be the same if I did go back? Of course not.'

'You can't go back, you can only go forward,' said Pat with the profundity arising from drink.

'We could go sideways,' I said.

'Yes, you one side, he the other,' Pat said.

'I can't bear to think about any of it,' I said.

Chris returned to London two days later in very high

spirits. Mine soon matched. Bobby, yet again, was shelved.

One afternoon, in the New Year, Chris and I were lying in bed, when my bell rang, loud, long and insistent.

'Ignore it,' said Chris, overriding any possible protest with a long kiss.

The bell rang again.

'Oh, God, who can it be?' I muttered. 'They sound pretty insistent.' I sat up in bed, debating rapidly the reasons why and why not I should answer it.

'It might be my mother,' I said.

'Can't you forget your mother, even at times like this?' Chris groaned.

'I shall have to answer.' I put my trousers and blouse on, kicking under the bed underclothes that had been scattered all over the room.

I opened the door and ran downstairs as the bell rang for the fourth time, whispering instructions to Chris to dress and straighten the bed.

When I opened the front door, I had a shock. There were two people there, on the point of turning away. One of them I didn't know, the other I did.

'Good God!' I gasped.

Lena laughed. 'I thought we'd surprise you. Can we come in? This is Thomas, by the way.'

'Hallo, Thomas,' I said. 'Come in, do. I'm so pleased to see you.'

I hardly needed to deploy delaying tactics, I was so surprised. Slowly I led the way up the stairs. Half-way up, I caught sight of my reflection in the mirror. My hair recorded accurately the fact that I had just got out of bed. My blouse was buttoned up wrongly and it was quite obvious that I had absolutely nothing on underneath it.

'This *is* a surprise!' I kept saying. 'I've never had a visit from the family. I'm ever so pleased to see you.'

When I showed Lena and Thomas into my room, Chris was sitting on the edge of the bed with an air of exaggerated innocence that told all. I glanced around. No evidence – apart from a bra strap peeping out from under the bedcover where it did not quite touch the floor. I reached out casually with my foot as I introduced Chris to Lena and Thomas.

Chris was slightly ill at ease, but I was determined not to let it bother me. I was so pleased to see Lena. And seeing Thomas, who was tall and black, explained everything. After my defection, Mother had obviously had even higher ambitions for Lena. Not only was Lena going to be a teacher – teachers being the only professional middle-class people we had regular contact with – she was going to marry well. And Mother's plans for Lena's intended did not include anything but a white skin.

'We're engaged,' Lena said excitedly, flashing what seemed a huge geological specimen at me. 'It's beautiful isn't it?'

It was indeed, and unconventional, citrine and pearls. I admired it and felt angry with Bobby for the common or garden sapphire and diamonds. I wondered if Chris would buy me a ring one day.

Thomas lived in London – hence Lena's train journey – and was the brother of one of her friends at college. He was studying law, but Lena did not think that would be enough for Mother, neither that nor the fact that he had been born in Britain. Wales to be exact, Cardiff. Mother hated the Welsh.

'Well,' I said, 'I don't know how much it's worth, but if you need some support when you go to break the news to Mother and Daddy, I could be there. Not,' I added darkly, 'that I think you deserve it, after landing me in it with Mother that time.'

Lena grinned. 'She was asking questions – why couldn't I come home for a whole weekend? That sort of thing. I just told her I saw you, that's all.' She paused, 'We're getting married. Soon. As soon as possible after we've told Mother and Daddy. Will you come?'

My hesitation was only brief but Lena noticed and turned quickly to Chris. 'And you as well, of course, Chris,' she added. Chris acknowledged the invitation coolly. Thomas looked bemused. Our mother, he must have been thinking, was going to have a difficult time with her daughters in the near future. If he, Thomas, was a problem, what would Chris be?

All four of us were busy with our own problems for a moment, then I offered more coffee to everyone and the atmosphere became relaxed. Chris, I noticed, though, was unusually quiet. I tried not to mind.

The next week I received another communication from Bobby. A postcard this time, with his address at the convent near Tunbridge Wells clearly written at the top. Chris, who by now was almost permanently resident in my room despite the single bed, saw the postcard: 'Please, *please* get in touch. I must discuss things with you.'

'Does he want you back?' asked Chris, voicing my fear with uncomfortable directness.

'I don't know,' I replied. 'He doesn't say so. He's still at the convent, not back at the flat. I don't know. I *hope* not.'

'Would you go if he did?'

'Of course not. I've got you!' I replied emphatically.

'What are you going to do, then?'

'I don't know.' Chris was obviously disturbed so I tried to be less vague. 'Go down and see him, I suppose.'

'When?'

I had to make a quick decision.

'Next Saturday.'

'Oh!' said Chris in a disappointed tone, to which I was expected to reply, 'what's the matter?'

I obliged. 'What's the matter?'

Chris shrugged. 'It's just that I'd planned to take you to

Brighton for the day. As a surprise.'

What a narrow escape! Fifty-odd miles of Chris's driving in each direction could have made a nervous wreck of me.

'Oh, I am sorry,' I was all concern that Chris's ego should not be deflated by my concern for a strange husband who lived in a convent and needed me. 'What a kind thought! But I really must go and see this wretched man or my conscience won't let me rest.'

'I always said religion was bad for you,' Chris said. 'I'll take you on Saturday.'

Tunbridge Wells must be half the distance of Brighton.

'You are a darling,' I said rewardingly and gave Chris kisses and cuddles to show my gratitude.

CHAPTER 15

Chris and I went together to the meeting of the group on Friday evening. Pat was there and so was the redoubtable Chloë Bidgood, with, I was amazed to see, a daughter of eight years old called Sophie. Sophie had light red hair, was pretty, precocious and, like her mother, did not expect to be ignored. I hated her on sight too.

'Bringing a child to a meeting like this,' I muttered as Chris and I left, pursing my lips and feeling just like Mother. 'At that age, a child should be in bed by eight and certainly not listening to the sort of problems we talk about. I felt unable to say some of the things I needed to say. What on earth is the woman thinking about?'

I burbled on in this vein, almost oblivious of Chris's difficulty in starting the car until a torrent of swear words alerted me to the problem.

I sat patiently while Chris fiddled about, in the boot, under the bonnet, not complaining about the bitter cold, the boredom and my shock at Chris's anger. After about fifteen minutes I was instructed to go back into the flat, where I told the tale of woe to the rest of the meeting, was given a mug of coffee and much sympathy. Several people went out to give Chris assistance and came back.

Eventually Chris returned and announced. 'Your hubby's

problem will have to wait. We can't go tomorrow. The Passion Wagon's totally kaput. And I haven't got any money to put her right.'

'Don't you belong to the RAC or the AA?' asked someone naívely.

Chris squashed them with a retort about the middle classes not knowing what poverty was. 'And if you wonder why I run such an expensive car, I'll tell you – it's my only extravagance. I don't drink, I don't smoke, I don't even have a telly. And now she won't even start!'

I knew better than to offer in public to lend Chris the money, or even contribute, so remained silent.

Chloë Bidgood asked if it was urgent that I saw Bobby.

'I think so,' I said, resenting her concern while grateful for her understanding. 'He hasn't told me what it's about. In fact, I haven't even seen him since I left. I can still go, on the coach or the train. I don't expect Chris will want to come with me though.'

'No,' said Chris shortly, 'you won't catch me on public transport not when I own a car like that.'

'I'll take you,' Chloë said, but not only to me, to the whole company. 'I'll take you tomorrow. Sophie and I were wondering what to do. I've never been to Tunbridge Wells. It'll be a day out. You'll want to come with Daff, won't you Chris? We'll make a day of it.'

I could have cursed Chloë Bidgood. I didn't want her, or her daughter, on my trip to see Bobby, but I did want Chris for support. And I knew Chris would have let me go alone if I went by bus or train. Public transport is *very* much beneath the dignity of the owner of a Sunbeam Rapier.

I feared that Chloë Bidgood was more interested in Chris than in my problems with Bobby.

The journey to Tunbridge Wells was somewhat reminiscent of travels with Mother and Daddy, Lena and Buster to see

Auntie Rose when I was small. In those days Lena always felt sick for the entire journey while Buster offered light relief with frequent requests to find a toilet.

On this occasion, it was Sophie who provided the punctuation of the journey. At Lewisham she was feeling sick, at Bromley she was sick. Somewhere between Bromley and Sevenoaks, she needed to go to the toilet at least three times. Though Chloë grumbled, we knew, and Sophie knew, it was a mere formality and Sophie's needs would be attended to. Because of Sophie's threats to be sick, Chloë avoided major roads and we made pleasant detours through villages and lanes, eventually getting lost. Chris's patience, which I now realized was limited, was being stretched to its absolute limits. It was with relief that we pulled into Sevenoaks for coffee and comfort. Chloë, clearly enjoying herself discovering Kent, decided to find out where she had been lost and to consult a map to avoid being lost again on the last leg of the journey. I suggested popping into the public library – a source of great and vital information at many bigger crisis-points in my life.

Chloë took up my suggestion immediately and single-mindedly led us to the public library. Sophie followed her, yelling 'Mum! Mum!' and I followed Sophie. Chris, emotionally reduced in status as a back-seat passenger in an aged Citroën Dyanne, followed me with a long-suffering scowl. In silence we looked up a Sophie-proof route from Sevenoaks to Tunbridge Wells and to the convent beyond.

We found the convent, eventually. It was attached to a large girls' school, in idyllic, story-book surroundings. Bobby's address we tracked down as being a tiny lodge at the main gate of the estate.

Chris, Chloë and Sophie drove through the village to get some refreshments at the pub. I was not too happy about leaving Chris in Chloë's clutches, nor at being deserted. I stood at the gate of the school, feeling miserable, lonely and frightened.

There was no answer from Bobby's house. Should I be pleased ot disappointed? I could not decide. Perhaps he was in the garden. I walked round the little house. The garden was small but was obviously being cared for. A pathetic pair of underpants and two pairs of socks on the line disturbed me. I peered through the latticed windows. The place was small, sparsely furnished but neat, tidy and totally deserted.

What should I do? I stared at the big school building at the end of the drive. My one desire was to run away, find the pub and Chris and return to London as quickly as possible and forget Bobby. But if I did that, I knew I would have to make the journey again – in Chris's Passion Wagon next time. That decided me. I began to hurry up the drive, running a short distance, then walking a little to regain some breath. I reached the man entrance and walked in. A nun came towards me and asked if she could help.

'Yes. I'm looking for Bobby Wright,' I panted, adding that I had come to visit him and he was not at home.

She frowned briefly, then seemed to recollect.

'Oh, yes. Wait here, dear. I'll inquire for you.'

She vanished. More nuns passed to and fro up and down the corridor, and several girls. There was that calm, off-white spaciousness of convent decor. I relaxed a little, resentfully.

I could see playing fields beyond the gardens – I remembered the old Catholic joke: if this is poverty, what is chastity like? I smiled to myself. I wanted to get back to Chris and share the thoughts in my mind as I waited in the convent.

My nun reappeared. 'I'm sorry dear,' she said kindly. 'He's out today. He's gone to London.'

I sat down again with an impatient sigh. 'I've come down *from* London to see him,' I said.

'I can always take a message and give to him when he returns.' she said. 'Whom shall I say wanted to see him?'

I looked her right in the eye. 'His wife,' I said.

As I had expected, she looked startled. 'Yes, very well dear,' she said. She was determined to be kind although I did not want her to be. 'I'll tell him you called.'

As I turned to leave, I softened. 'Sister,' I said, 'what is he doing here?'

'He's our gardener, dear,' she said.

'Oh. I see.' I smiled at her at last. 'Thank you. If you would tell him, please, I'd be grateful.'

I ran and walked back down the drive, out the gate with barely a glance at the little cottage that was Bobby's home and rushed through the village to the pub and to Chris. They were sitting in a rear lounge, eating ploughman's lunches and drinking lager. Sophie was plunging her sticky fingers into an enormous bag of crisps and slurping coke through a straw.

They all paused and looked at me questioningly.

'How did you get on?' Chloë ventured at last.

'Silly idiot has gone to London for the day,' I said.

Chris looked cross.

We drove back to London in a much quieter atmosphere than on the outward journey. I hardly spoke. Chris hardly spoke. Chloë had less to say than she would have done had we been more responsive. Sophie did not feel sick, nor threaten to be sick. Despite a huge consumption of coke, she did not once ask to stop the car because she wanted to go to the toilet. I spent the journey wondering what Chris had said to Chloë during my absence. Chloë was not the sort of person to sit quietly and be ignored. No one who wore a scarlet track-suit and dangling earrings to match could be ignored. I thought Chris liked her and I thought her attraction lay not only in her vibrant personality, but in her frankly unsophisticated and uneducated background, which she wore as an asset. Chris, being totally unacademic, wholly practical in ability and sensitive about being unemployed, must surely have seen Chloë as a kindred spirit.

So when Chloë suggested going back to her place for a

meal before completing the final leg of the journey across London to my place in Hampstead, I was neither surprised nor pleased when Chris accepted for both of us.

Chloë lived in the East End, in a large Victorian terraced house in a street of identical houses. The house had been left to her by her parents and some of the year was lived in by a rich aunt who spent most of her time and money on travel. She was at present spending the winter in Greece. I thought that people in the East End were poor. Perhaps this was yet another of Mother's prejudices that I had inherited. Certainly, Chloë's comfortably furnished house did not indicate any lack of money, with its fitted carpets, central heating, wall-lights, expensive net curtains and labour-saving aids. Mother, in her long-suffering poverty and reluctant socialism would not have recognized Chloë's militancy and affluence as having anything in common with her own life.

Chloë's hospitality was as extravagant as her way of dressing and living. While Sophie sat motionless before the television, she concocted, on the spot, a spaghetti Bolognaise, serving it with a bottle of wine in a dining-room of Ercol furniture.

Chris was unusually subdued. Perhaps it was the spaghetti. I always found spaghetti a bit of a problem and spent a lot of time concentrating on not slurping it, worm by worm, through pursed lips, leaving little orange splashes all down my front. I thought Chris might be similarly embarrassed. Or was the dreadful Sophie, unself-consciously slurping spaghetti, splashing herself, the table-cloth and everyone else with little orange spots, and actually laughing about it, the source of Chris's discomfiture? Or was it me?

'Have you got any plans for the evening?' Chloë inquired innocently.

I had hoped to return home and go to bed early, but I was beginning to doubt my assumption that Chris was of like mind.

'Well, I think we ought to get back,' Chris said before Chloë could suggest alternatives. 'But don't bother about a lift. We can go on the bus.'

'Are you sure?' Chloë was concerned. 'It's no trouble really.'

'We'll go by bus,' Chris said curtly.

Chloë seemed offended and Chris seemed not to care. The atmosphere on the way home was heavy.

Waiting for me when we arrived was a letter from Lena. In it was a wedding invitation for me and Chris – Lena and Thomas were to be married in a month's time. Mother had been presented with a *fait accompli* and. apart from an anxious inquiry as to the reason for the apparent haste to be married, Lena said, hardly batted an eyelid.

'Oh, I'm so pleased!' I told Chris as I put the kettle on for coffee. 'I feel as though I'm more or less back in the family again. I really did think she might not ask me, me being such a disgrace, and all that.' I hesitated. 'You will come, won't you, Chris?'

Chris looked away from me. 'I don't know.'

My stomach turned over. What was this? What had I done? I tried the gentle approach first, but Chris was deaf to sympathy.

'Well, I don't know what's the matter with you if you don't tell me,' I said impatiently. 'I'm not going to spend the rest of the evening trying to guess what your problem is. You can either tell me, or forget it.'

'It's all right for you,' Chris grumbled.

'Oh, yes. It's lovely for me. You've been like this all day. I don't know what it's about. Do you want to come to the wedding or not?'

'No.'

I was hurt. 'But why not?'

Chris turned to look at me at last. 'Because I'll feel a fish out of water. It's bound to be posh.'

'What? My lot?' I was incredulous.

Chris looked at me as though I was unutterably dim. 'A teacher? A lawyer?'

'Oh.' I was unable to consider Lena as posh.

'And you're all religious.'

'I'm not any more,' I pointed out.

We were both silent. I drank my coffee and nibbled biscuits to keep me calm. I could not understand why Chris was in such a mood. I began to feel frightened. Was Chris perhaps not merely interested in Chloë Bidgood, but deeply involved? I must ask, I did so nervously.

Chris's dismissive laugh was no comfort. 'Chloë Bidgood? you must be joking!'

'Are you worried about the car?'

'Of course I'm worried about the bloody car. I'm worried about money. I'm worried about not getting a job. Wouldn't you be?'

'Why don't you train for something, then? There's plenty of things you could do.'

'Yes, I know,' Chris nodded. 'I could learn a skill, like carpentry. I could do a social worker's course. I don't know what I want to do.' Chris calmed down a bit and turned to me looking desperate. 'Daff, I don't know what I want to be. I don't know whether to be a carpenter or a social worker.'

No response at all seemed to be the wisest choice to this appeal. I wanted to laugh. Like Auntie Rose, I could see the funny side. I had a husband who couldn't decide between the sacred and the secular, and now a lover who couldn't decide whether to be working class and proud of it or to identify with the aspiring middle classes.

The silence became agonizingly long. I stood up and paced the room. Something was wrong, terribly wrong. What had I done? Was I expecting too much? Was I too demanding? Was I just hopeless at relating to people? Was I a problem?

'Look Chris,' I said, close to tears, 'I can't stand this. If I've done or said something, tell me.'

'Nope,' said Chris.

'Well, what is it?'

Chris shrugged.

'Are you fed-up with me?'

Chris shrugged again.

'Do you think I'm fed up with you?'

Again the shrug, and then there was another long silence.

'Daff,' said Chris tentatively. 'How broad-minded are you?'

Broad-mindedness was now something I prided myself on. 'Very,' I said.

'If I tell you something, promise not to be angry?'

Rashly I promised.

'The truth is,' Chris said, 'I want to change sex.'

CHAPTER 16

Another crisis. My life was full of them. What on earth was I to do now? Chris had gone home, upset. I sat in my room, upset, and spent a full half hour contemplating the damage and destruction I had perpetrated on myself in my quest for – what? – sex! My internalized mother gave me a good telling off and suggested that I should give up this passion for passion. Go back to Bobby – if he would have me, if I could find him. What a mess!

Maureen was whooping it up in the next room. Silly woman, I thought. Doesn't she know there are other things in life?

Like what?

If only someone would tell me!

Perhaps there was something wrong with me – something other than what I had already discovered. Perhaps my dreadful fate was to leap from lover to lover in the same manner as I had jumped from job to job when I left school. But that had been, I discovered, to punish my mother. Who was I punishing now? There was only me left, and I had not known, when we met, that Chris was transsexual. I had a sneaking suspicion that, had I really loved Chris, it would not have mattered whether he or she was male or female.

Now I was beginning to feel certain there was something

wrong with me. I thought back fleetingly to Wendy, whose dreadful fate had been to become pregnant out of wedlock at eighteen. Rumour had it, and was spread eagerly by Lena on her recent visit, that in addition to the first baby, Wendy was now the proud mother of twins, married to Brian Jones and living in a beautiful detached house on the edge of the town. She was also very fat.

That, I thought, could have been me. There obviously was something else in life besides sex, and it was money. But I was too much of a prude to want to get involved with that.

After half an hour of such critical self-examination and soul-searching, I put my coat on and went round to Pat's.

Pat was in, grieving over a brief but broken love affair. I thought we would comfort each other. But I was mistaken. Pat's eyes gleamed.

'Jesus, Mary and Joseph! he said. 'Transsexual. The operation. Hormone tablets. How exciting. I've never met a transsexual before. Daff, old thing, you have all the luck!'

'I suppose that's one way of looking at it,' I said, 'but I don't quite feel it's a status symbol. I feel I've let Chris down. I'm fickle, Pat and I'll end up like Wendy Robinson, or worse, thinking that life is all about money.'

'You mean it isn't?' Pat said, 'And me working me guts out day in day out.'

'Don't tease,' I said.

'Well, come on, Daff. Be realistic. To most people, life is about sex, money or religion. Make your choice.'

'I have. I thought it was about sex. I didn't know, though, that sex was about letting other people use you or, worse still, me using other people.'

Pat laughed heartily. 'Grow up, Daff. Where did you get your romantic notions?'

There was only one source. 'From Mother, I suppose, I should have known *she* was wrong. What on earth do I do now?'

'Stop the search,' Pat advised. 'And if we are both still disillusioned in a couple of years time, we'll both get married – to each other.'

I smiled. 'A proposal? Life can't be too bad, can it?'

Pat split the bed up, and I stayed the night, sleeping on the mattress on the floor. We talked in the darkness and I told of the journey to Tunbridge Wells, of Chloë Bidgood's awful offspring, Sophie, of the convent and Bobby not being there.

'And,' I finished fiercely, 'if Bobby wants to see me, he can jolly well write and make arrangements to come and see *me*. I'm not traipsing all the way to Tunbridge Wells again.'

'That's the stuff,' said Pat, sleepily.

We spent the next day together, moaning, supporting coaxing and drinking. The consequence was that when I awoke on Monday morning I had a massive hangover. So I rang work to say I was 'throwing up'. That guaranteed that they would be glad not to see me near the place for at least two days.

By the afternoon I felt better so I went out for a walk in the pale winter sunshine and sharp air to clear my head.

I wandered into a newsagents looking for inspiration but only found women's magazines, which I could not afford if I was going to eat for the rest of the week. I flicked through them, though, and scanned the agony columns for information on transsexuals, or a hint on what my problem could be. I recalled my rigid adherence to advice in agony columns in my younger days when I was at what now seemed to be the very beginning of my quest for knowledge about sex. I recalled, also my researches in the public library. With this in mind I replaced the magazine, strode out of the shop, down the road and into the public library.

I made straight for the psychology section. I couldn't decide what to look for first, transsexuality or my nameless problem. I thought I'd be generous and deal with Chris's problem first as I felt I had been unjust to Chris in not falling in love with him or her. But I learned nothing from the books that Chris had not told me. I toyed with the idea of going to the desk and asking where to find books on . . . what? Sexology? but my nerve failed me.

I mooched around the library looking for help, direction, some answer to my problems, some name to my problems.

I found it. Just as I was giving up and was on my way out, in fact. There was a notice, pinned up in the entrance hall, done by hand, in eye-catching purple and green letters.

Women's Group
Meets every Monday 7.00 p.m.
Women's Centre

and it gave the address and telephone number of the women's centre.

I memorized the address. This was it. This was the answer, I thought. This was my problem – well, situation. Men were the cause of it all. I hated them. Nervous though I was, I vowed I would go to the meeting that evening. The promise of action calmed my mind.

Of course, I had it all wrong, hadn't I? For a start, I had dressed up, put on my best skirt and jumper, tights and the highest heels I had ever possessed, at least one and a half inches. But they were one and a half inches too high . . .

The Women's Centre was in a run-down street in a run-down area. Later I learned that it was reputed to be a 'red light' district and had I known this at the time, I would not have gone to the meeting at all, let alone stood in the doorway of the deserted centre for five minutes.

The centre was an empty shop, above which hung a big board proclaiming the virtues of the premises and announcing that it was To Let.

I stood in the dark doorway of the centre, reading the

notices plastered on the inside of the window. As well as having my consciousness raised, I could learn to defend myself with Judo, join a campaign against contraceptive injections or become a member of a prostitutes' self-help group. The latter startled me somewhat, not having any idea why prostitutes might need help. I could learn carpentry, or upholstery or join a women's rock group if I could play the guitar. The options did not fill me with wild excitement, but at least they were new.

A figure appeared in the doorway, holding a bunch of keys.

'Hello,' she said. 'Have you come to join us this evening?'

'Yes,' I said. 'If that's OK.'

'It's very OK,' said the stranger, pushing the door open for me to enter the dark building.

'We're looking for new members.' She turned and shouted over her shoulder. 'Fanny, we've got a new member!'

'Oh, great,' called back Fanny.

'My name's Lou,' said the woman as she felt around in the dark for the light switch. 'Ah! There. We can see now. What's your name?'

After Fanny and Lou, Daffodil sounded quite ordinary, so I confessed.

I looked around the centre. The shop front was small and its windows covered with posters. There were tables with leaflets on everything from welfare rights to self-defence, peace to battered wives. The amount of information was overwhelming and served to illustrate my ignorance on my rights and position as a woman.

Behind the shop front was a small room with pannelled walls. Lou was plugging in an electric fire. I sat down on a rickety sofa and tried to straighten out a ruck in the threadbare carpet. Lou left the room with a kettle. Fanny came in carrying milk and sugar, which she put on a table in the corner. She smiled at me warmly. Her calm relaxed expression and manner were a contrast to the way she dressed and spoke. For someone so pretty, I could not help feeling that her deliberate attempts to look impoverished were a pity. She had on a long cotton skirt that was faded and limp; cheap, thick socks of dark green; flat regulation school sandals; and a long purple jumper whose cuffs came over her fingers. Round her neck were two scarves, limp, with fringes, and her hair, bushy and frizzy had long since outgrown a perm.

Lou had disappeared to the back of the shop. I could hear a lavatory chain being pulled rhythmically about ten times. Fanny laughed and explained.

'It works perfectly once you've got the knack,' she said.

Lou returned with the full kettle. 'Tea or coffee?' she said plugging in and arranging cups.

'Oh, coffee, please,' I said. I was feeling dumb and overdressed.

Lou's style in clothes was similar to Fanny's, but tidier. She had black stockings or tights and black shoes and a black jumper in contrast to a red skirt. She looked like a stylish peasant.

We drank coffee and I asked polite questions about the Women's Centre. I felt awkward. They knew it. I resented their attempts to put me at ease.

Eventually I had to visit the lavatory and learn to 'pull ten times and hope.' Outside the lavatory was a flight of stairs going down to a basement. On my return to the little pannelled room, I asked what was down there.

'That's the basement,' said Fanny. 'We have parties and things down there. It's quite big. A lot of space. It used to be the workshop.'

'Workshop?' I asked.

'Yes, where they made the coffins. This used to be an undertaker's.'

I stared at her in horror. She laughed. I gazed round at the pannelled walls.

This was the Chapel of Rest,' said Lou, reading my thoughts.

What am I doing here? I asked myself. What am I doing, in a slummy undertaker's, sitting on dilapidated furniture, drinking appalling coffee with two obviously educated young women simulating poverty?

My thoughts were interrupted by a banging on the door and shouts and laughter from outside.

'It's Caroline,' said Lou, springing up.

Caroline entered. She was large, dressed in black, waterproof motor-cycle gear, which she commenced to peel off as she recounted the difficulties of her journey to the Women's Centre.

'Oh, a new member!' she exclaimed, placing her helmet on the floor. 'Who are you?'

'I'm Daffodil,' I said.

'Daffodil!' snorted Caroline. 'That's not your real name, is it? You're not like Fanny, are you, trying to make a point?'

'No. It's my real name. What do you mean?' I turned to Fanny.

'Caroline laughs at me because I call myself Fanny these days. She doesn't understand that I have a one-woman mission to fight against the denigration of the female genitals.'

I blushed in my embarrassment. They were so forthright.

Caroline laughed at my expression. 'It's a 'Fannies are beautiful' campaign.'

'Yes, I'm sure they are,' I said. I dared not ask what Lou's mission in life was.

With the arrival of Caroline, the meeting began in earnest. Last week, apparently, they had been discussing Caroline's problems with her boyfriend and they continued to do so this week. I was not able to follow the discussion very well and could not figure out what Caroline's problem was. Then Fanny, somehow, became the focus because she was having a similar but different conflict with her girlfriend. Fanny, I gathered after some minutes, liked ladies. Several times they turned to me and asked my opinion and I tried to respond helpfully. They were kind about my offerings. When it transpired that Lou was not sure how to describe her sexuality, I chipped in with surprise and sympathy.

'I don't understand,' I said, 'how you can't be sure. Perhaps you're bisexual.'

'That's what we decided ages ago,' Lou said, 'but it's not as easy as that. Am I heterosexual and lesbian at the same time, or alternately, and, if alternately, how long am I each for, and how do I know when I change? And what about long-term relationships? It's difficult.'

'Put that way,' I said, 'it sounds impossible. Mind you,' I added, certain that this would interest them, 'I was closely involved with a transsexual. I thought *that* was almost impossible.'

Three pairs of eyes focused on me.

'Male or female?' asked Caroline.

I giggled wittily. 'Yes!'

'No, seriously, was it a male or female, going to female or male?'

'Oh, I see.' I felt important. 'It was a woman, wanting to be a man.'

'How did you feel about it?' Lou asked. 'You said you were "closely" involved. Did you mean you were in a relationship with this person?'

'Oh, yes,' I replied going pink. 'But I can't cope with it. I was sort of "in love with love" if you know what I mean. I've ended it. I know it was cruel, but I couldn't cope.'

There was a sympathetic silence. Then Fanny spoke again.

'Of course, the female to male transsexual doesn't cause as much interest in the public imagination for two reasons – it's taken for granted that all women envy men and want to be like them, and also, it's much more salacious to think of cutting off a penis than sticking one on. It's sort of . . . well, daring. A penis is sacred.'

'Yes, I know!' I burst out. 'When I was little, I touched my brother's willie when he was lying in his pram. My mother said "Oh, you must never touch that!" So I don't.'

They laughed and wanted to know what I meant by my last brief sentence. Before I could explain, there was an urgent banging on the door.

'It's only me!' a familiar voice called through the letter-box.

Lou sprang up to let the newcomer in. Who should it be but Chloë Bidgood.

Chloë, resplendent in swirling Indian cotton, silk scarves and dangling earrings, swept in looking like Katherine Hepburn with glasses, and was equally amazed to see me.

Once Chloë had arrived, there was no hope of the discussion continuing. Chloë took over, in the nicest possible way, and was never serious. When told that we had been on the point of discussing the sacredness of penises, she roared with laughter, not because she thought they were sacred, or because she thought they weren't, but because, as she said, 'Every time I come here, to a *women's* meeting, mark you Daffodil, we are discussing *men*. The joke is, only Caroline actually lives with one, and only Caroline is definitely heterosexual!'

'Yes, but Chloë,' Fanny said quietly, 'all of us – except Daffodil, as far as I know – have definitely had relationships with men.'

'So has Daffodil,' said Chloë, before I could speak up for myself. 'So has Daffodil, haven't you, Daff? Tell them, Daff, about your husband. Tell them you've got a husband who's in a convent!'

The other three looked at me with renewed interest.

'You're a dark horse,' said Lou.

'What's your husband's problem?' Caroline asked bluntly.

'Religion,' I said.

'Oh!' Caroline was disappointed.

'I wondered if he had gender identity problems,' said Lou seriously.

'He wants to be a monk,' I said. I felt I had to defend Bobby. 'He's a gardener at a convent. I know it sounds funny.'

'It's not him who sounds funny,' said Chloë. 'It's you, thank God. I can't take all this earnestness. Life's too short. Who's coming to the pub?'

Fanny and Lou looked disapproving in a charitable way and referred to public houses as being male preserves.

'Well, we'll alter that in one pub for one evening,' announced Chloë. 'Come on. I can't stand this place. It's as cold as a morgue and about as cheerful.'

We allowed ourselves to be ushered from the Women's Centre to a warm but male-dominated pub a few turnings away. There we commandeered a corner, monopolized the fruit-machine and talked and laughed loudly. Chloë demanded and achieved the same service at the bar as the men who propped it up.

'See?' she said. 'Pretend they don't exist, like they do us.'

I could see that Lou and Fanny did not agree with her philosophy, but enjoyed her way of putting it into practice. Caroline was just amused. I, frankly, began to hate Chloë Bidgood less and admire her more. She asked me how Chris was, so I told her the whole story. She listened.

'It doesn't surprise me,' she said, 'Chris always struck me as being a bit, well, butch, and somewhat lacking in confidence. I hope she comes through it all OK, if she's determined to go through with it.'

'Oh she is,' I said. 'She's seeing her GP today.'

'I expect it's all very upsetting for you,' Chloë suggested.

'Very. I haven't been to work today. I phoned in to say I was throwing up. I reckoned they'd be only too glad not to see me if I said that.'

'That's a good one,' Chloë said. 'I must remember that when the old back-trouble story wears a bit thin.'

'So what've you done with Sophie tonight?' I asked.

Chloë made a face. 'I'm cut up about Sophie at the moment. She's living with Daddy. I have her at weekends. She used to live with me until he kept her on an access visit.'

Personally, I could not imagine either Sophie's mother or her father wanting to have her live with them and thought it very loving and motherly of Chloë to want to have her daughter.

Chloë told me all about her husband and how the marriage broke up and by the time we had finished exchanging confidences and commiserations, Lou, Fanny and Caroline had left. Chloë gave me a lift home. Outside my house, she pointed to the Catholic church across the road.

'That's where I was married,' she said.

'You're not a Catholic, are you?' I asked.

She said she was.

'So am I,' I said. 'Or was. I've joined the ranks of the lapsed.'

'Me too,' she said. 'You know, I've often thought I'd like to join Quandary.'

'What on earth is that?'

'The group for Catholics – of our bent, so to speak. I think it's mainly men, though. If I find out when and where it is, shall we go one evening?'

'OK,' I said. 'Sounds like an appropriate name – Quandary.'

CHAPTER 17

Pat felt very threatened by my involvement with the women's movement.

'I know what's going to happen to you now,' he predicted, as we drank our lunch in the pub the next day, 'You're going to get all anti-men. You'll have nothing to do with me and I'll be left all alone with me misery.'

'No you won't,' I said. 'It's just that I'm not going to be a willie-worshipper any more.'

'You never were!'

'Well, it's official now. And it won't make any difference to our friendship.'

'D'you mean that?'

'Of course!'

'Jesus, Mary and Joseph! I thought for a while all the fun was going out of me working life. You do realize, don't you Daff, that they all think we're having an affair?'

This was amusing news.

'Do they really? Then don't let's spoil their fun. We'll walk back arm in arm.'

I continued to go to the meetings at the Women's Centre every Monday. We always seemed to talk about sex at these meetings. I asked Chloë to check whether my perceptions were becoming distorted.

'Do you always talk about sex?' I asked.

'Is there anything else?' she countered.

'That's what I want to know,' I said.

I also continued my attendance at the Friday evening group. I saw Chloë at both meetings and when she suggested that we attend a Quandary meeting one Wednesday evening, I felt I had a very full social life indeed. I wrote to tell Auntie Rose as much to make sure she knew I was not lonely.

'Do you know,' said Chloë as we drove to our Quandary venue, 'I get sick and tired of meetings in sleezy premises. That flat of Michael's that we go to every Friday is like a kitchen-sink stage set. That Women's Centre really *is* a morgue. I dread to think what we're in for tonight. Some pimply ex-seminarian's impoverished bed-sitter, I expect. Honestly, when you've grown up in the East End like I have, you fight against shabbiness. Do you feel the same, Daff?'

'Well, no,' I confessed. 'But then, I grew up within sight of trees and green fields and things. I feel, when I find myself in these places, that I'm experiencing Real Life.'

Chloë snorted impatiently. We drew up before a big red-brick block of flats in a smart area of London. Chloë had been quite wrong about the impoverished bed-sitter.

We were welcomed into a large room, where everything from the carpet to the tobacco and cigar smoke was thick. There were some dozen or so well-dressed men standing around talking in loud voices. They were surprised but delighted to see us.

'We don't often have ladies at our meeting,' said one of them named Adam.

'Ladies?' said Chloë stiffly. 'I'm no lady. We're women, aren't we Daff?'

I did not understand this appeal for solidarity but I agreed with her. She perched on the arm of a leather armchair.

'Why don't you have many women at these meetings?' she asked.

'I don't know really,' said Adam frowning.

'Yes, we do, you know we do!' A hand appeared on Adam's shoulder and a face peered over it and introduced itself as Roger.

'We do, Adam, really. You should tell them.'

'About the group, you mean?' Adam frowned again. 'But are they "official"? I mean, I know we're not, really, but we're more "official" than they are.'

'But the girls should know. Perhaps Chloë and Daffodil don't want to be official, either.'

Chloë turned to me and muttered, 'Isn't it amazing how even men who are not interested in women still have to impress us?'

I had not realized that that was what had been going on, but now that Chloë had opened my eyes I had to acknowledge that it was a very plausible theory.

'What is this other group?' Chloë said. 'Is it for . . .' she paused, 'girls?'

'Oh, it's called the Faithful Companions of Ruth and Naomi, I think,' said Adam, not wanting to betray the boys. 'They were a group of women who belonged to Quandary but broke away to form their own group.'

'Why did they do that?' Chloë insisted.

'Because they didn't like men,' said Adam with a pained look. Roger made an exasperated sound.

'It wasn't *really* that. They got fed up with us. One of them said she felt we expected her to make the tea and coffee,' Roger explained.

'I thought it was because one of them wanted us to agree with her that women should be allowed to be priests,' Adam said. 'Ridiculous!'

Clearly Roger did not agree with Adam. A third man, Christopher, joined us and began explaining to us the reason why women cannot be ordained in the Catholic church. It all boiled down, in the end, to biology.

'One of the conditions for entry into the priesthood,' Christopher expounded broad-mindedly, 'is that you have to have testicles!'

Chloë stood up, tilted her head to one side, 'Do they have to be your own – or can they be anybody's?' she asked.

The meeting was quite interesting. A priest gave a talk on morals and sexuality. I was surprised to hear some of the things he said, it appeared that the church was as ambivalent about me – and people like me – as I was about the church. But Chloë was in a denigrating mood.

'No wonder the women left,' she said. 'They don't take women seriously there. What does a celibate priest know about women and sex? And they are so middle class.' She said it as though being middle class was a distinct drawback.

'What's wrong with that?' I asked naïvely, and Chloë gave me another lecture on what it had been like growing up in the East End.

'And they are so *male*,' she said.

'I had noticed,' I said. 'I'm afraid I'm not a very good feminist.'

'And I'm not a very good Catholic. If I track down this Ruth and Naomi lot, will you come to a meeting with me?'

My consciousness was being raised – rapidly.

The next big event in my life was Lena's wedding. I took Pat with me. I thought his presence might confuse the family.

Unlike Rita's wedding, this one and my frame of mind did not call for a red chiffon dress. I wore a blue wool dress, with last year's winter coat and looked and felt quite unremarkable. I needed to. This was going to be a minor ordeal.

Mother was suffering. With one daughter entering a marriage which she did not approve of, and the other having left a marriage of which she did approve, Mother was in her own private little quandary without any support. Daddy, of course, was quite happy for Lena to marry Thomas, and for me to leave Bobby, as well as for me to make my own way in life in accordance with who I was. And if I did insist on bringing a man to the wedding, just to confound and confuse all the relatives, especially Mother, well, all the better. Relatives of that sort needed confounding and confusing. His side of the family were such a mixed bunch, he was only too glad to see Lady Mulligan punished for her snobbery over his family.

So I had a lovely welcome from Daddy and so did Pat, whom I introduced as a good friend from Cork.

Lena was radiant, totally aware of the various undercurrents, but able to rise above them all. Thomas's family was large, so there were four black bridesmaids in pink dresses and two pink bridesmaids in blue dresses. They all looked lovely and, unlike at mine and Bobby's wedding, the sun shone, dresses stayed in one piece, the cake was beautiful and Mother not quite so smug. I took all this to be a good omen for Lena and Thomas.

Father Terry officiated. The choir had sung beautifully, led by Sebastian of course, and Dolores, by special request from Lena, sang a solo – Gounod's 'Ave Maria'. Pat, who had heard of all these people during my interminable retelling of my story, was interested to have them all identified.

'And over there,' I said, 'in the blue hat in the choir, is Dolores, the woman I fell in love with.'

I had a few words with Lena at the reception. This was held in the church hall and was a really splendid affair, in comparison to mine. Mother took all the credit. She also took a lot of bullying from Lena, I think.

'Mother is in a mood,' Lena said. 'Has been for weeks. She can't cope, you know. The cupboard is so full now, of skeletons she can't shut the door.'

'Skeletons?'

'You. Me. And there's the little story about herself she told me.'

'Herself?'

'Don't stand there repeating what I say!' Lena laughed. 'I expect you don't know. But she's tried to put so many skeletons in her cupboard, now the lot have come tumbling out.'

'What do you mean?' I breathed, sensing scandal.

Lena looked over towards Grandma who, at eighty-something was doing a passable imitation of Queen Victoria. Dressed smartly in navy blue, she sat with rigid back and head lifted surveying the guests from beneath lowered eyelids. Her hands rested on her lap.

'Grandad,' Lena whispered, 'was not our grandfather. Mother was illegitimate.'

'Never!' I gasped. 'So we're not the grandchildren of a Welsh postman?' I was disappointed.

'No. According to Auntie Rose – and I'm not supposed to know this – we're probably the grandchildren of an Irish priest.'

That was better than a Welsh postman. Furthermore, Mother's name before she married had not been Smith. It had been Gotobed.

I couldn't help it. I let out a very unrefined snigger.

'With a name like that,' I commented to Lena, 'you have to live up to it, or deny it. Poor Mother!'

I went straight over to Pat to tell him.

'Chloë,' I said, 'will just love that when I tell her.'

I saw Auntie Rose, Uncle Wack and Ritchie. Ritchie was showing an interest in one of the bridesmaids. He was seventeen now and had grown up to be quiet and serious. Curious though I was, this did not seem to be the occasion on which to ascertain whether Auntie Rose was Mother's half-sister or not. It was far too delicate a matter and needed time – preferably a fortnight at Auntie Rose's for my summer holiday.

Apart from Mother trying hard to ignore me, and Buster

actually succeeding in doing so, my day at Lena's wedding was quite a success until just before Lena and Thomas were about to leave for their honeymoon. Who should walk in, pink, embarrassed and with a book on marriage annulment tucked under his arm, but Bobby!

'Hallo, Daff,' he said. What else was there to say after months of desertion?

'Hallo, Bobby,' I said, thinking what the hell are you doing here?

'How are you?' he said.

'I'm fine,' I said, lying womanfully. 'How are you?'

'I'm fine.'

I knew everybody was looking at us, expecting either the grand reconciliation with us falling, sobbing into each other's arms, or the final parting, fists and tempers flying. I knew Bobby was capable of neither, and I certainly was not going to satisfy anybody's expectations with a solo performance. I wanted to comment on his clothes – jeans and sweater, so unlike the Bobby I had married, but I kept quiet. Fancy turning up at a wedding like that, I thought. But Bobby had always been rather unworldly. He now seemed totally unaware of the social gaffe he had made.

'I must talk to you,' he said.

Mother came bearing down on us with her barracuda smile, all teeth and no mirth.

'Hallo, Bobby dear,' she said, emphasizing every word. She spoke loudly. No one would be in any doubt that she was the fondest of mothers-in-law. It was, clearly, all Daffodil's fault that the marriage had broken up.

'Hallo,' said Bobby. 'I just popped in. I couldn't get here earlier. Thanks for inviting me.'

'Not at all, dear,' said Mother, 'I think you *should* be here. You are one of the family – still.'

This last word was said with a sidelong glance at me.

'I want to talk to Daff,' Bobby said.

'Of course you do.' Mother patted him on the shoulder. Optimism wafted from her in waves.

At this moment, Lena and Thomas appeared. I must say, by this time Lena did not deserve the nickname she had been given as a child. She was elegant.

Her bouquet came flying through the air, the bridesmaids clammering for it. It hit me fair and square on the side of my face. Mother surely thought it a good omen.

Bobby and I found a quiet corner in which to talk. He thrust at me the book he had been carrying. It was called *Marriage Annulment.* Whatever happened to monasteries?

'I must talk to you,' he said.

I pointed out that he was.

'I've been reading this book. It's about marriage annulment in the church.'

'So I see,' I remarked.

'I've been wondering if we have any grounds for annulling our marriage,' he said. 'Then I can join an Order.'

'What about me?' I asked.

'You can get married again. Properly.'

'Oh,' I said, 'had you anyone in mind for me?'

I knew what annulment meant. The church, under certain circumstances can declare that a marriage did not exist. It is better than civil divorce. It lets you off the hook completely, no guilty party, no marriage even.

'Daff, do listen. I want you to borrow this book and tell me if you think we have any reason to believe our marriage didn't exist. I'd like to be right with the church.'

I pushed the book back.

'Honestly, Bobby, I don't think this is the right occasion to discuss such matters. And I don't really want to discuss them anywhere. If you must, you can get in touch. You know my address. Take your book back. I'm going home, now.'

From the corner of my eye, I had seen Father Terry appear. I was not anxious to meet him. I found Pat and we set off back to London.

CHAPTER 18

On Monday, at work, I had two personal telephone calls. The voice of the first caller I could not identify at first, yet it seemed very familiar.

'You don't recognize me, do you?' said the voice. 'What a short memory Daffodil Mulligan. And we were so close. You're fickle.'

I didn't like being called fickle. I did not like being teased, either. It began to sound like one of those unpleasant, anonymous phone calls that telephonists sometimes receive. The heavy breathing would follow next. Yet how did he know my name?

'It's not Chris, is it?' I said. 'It's Chris' I was pleased but uneasy. How does one deal with an ex-lover who is changing sex? It was easy to be angry with Bobby in a dignified way. But this was different.

Chris was pleased at being recognized. 'I'm on the tablets,' Chris explained. 'I feel great. I pass as a man, now. I'm Christopher, not Christobel.'

I giggled. 'I never knew you *were* Christobel. It's worse then Daffodil!'

'For me, it was impossible. Anyway, it's full steam ahead with the operations and everything. I've got an appointment with a psychiatrist next week.'

'Psychiatrist?'

'Just a precaution. It's the way it's done. By the way, I phoned Chloë earlier. She's going to phone you about some Catholic group you're interested in. Honestly, you Catholics are a laugh. I don't understand you.'

I don't understand you either, I wanted to say, but did not want to be hurtful. Chris asked me how I was getting on and I explained about Bobby and Lena's wedding and mentioned Quandary, and the women's group. Then Chris said, 'No hard feelings, eh, Daff?'

'No,' I said, surprised. 'No, Of course not. I thought you might be feeling a bit well – resentful, of me.'

'No,' growled Chris. ''Course not. I think you're a smasher, Daff.'

Chloë rang later to say that she had tracked down the Faithful Companions of Ruth and Naomi. They had a meeting the following Sunday in North London, and would I go with her? I agreed before she revealed that the horrible Sophie, on an access visit, would be accompanying us.

The meeting of the Faithful Companions of Ruth and Naomi was held in a dreary church hall. A piece of paper drawing-pinned to the street door, had a mysterious insignia 'FCRN' and an upward-pointing arrow on it. We took this to mean that the meeting was upstairs, so pushed open the door. There was a flight of stairs. At the top was another door with another piece of paper pinned to it. 'FCRN – Please Enter'. Sophie giggled. Chloë glared at her.

We pushed open the second door. Inside was a high room, very gloomy, with dull stained-glass windows, wooden panelled walls and floors covered with well-flattened carpet tiles. Seated on the floor in a circle were about a dozen women. None of them turned as we entered, but all continued to gaze at a single candle in the centre of their circle. We stood staring, not speaking, and I wondered whether to turn and leave. I glanced at Chloë doubtfully. She shrugged and mouthed 'Meditation', at me. A woman wearing a nun's veil turned her attention to us and indicated that we should sit down on the floor near her. She smiled. I smiled back, not certain if it was the correct thing to do. I could see Chloë hesitating, so I took hold of Sophie's hand and crept to the spot the nun had indicated. I sat cross-legged on the floor. Sophie copied me eagerly. Chloë made a face and tried to tuck her legs before her comfortably but found it difficult.

The room was utterly still. I tried to put myself in the correct frame of mind. I had read about meditation but was not sure now what to do. My uncertainty was increased by the lack of information as to how long I was expected to sit like this.

I decided to meditate upon my fellow human beings. None of them appeared to be aware that I was looking at them. They were of all ages from about twenty to sixty. Some were fat, some thin, some pretty, some just plain and homely. The nun was in her thirties and had a long, thin face and long thin hair. She looked very earnest, and I thought how compassionate of her to take an interest in people like us. So few did.

Chloë fidgeted. Her long legs were a problem. Also, she was not the sort of person to sit still and inactive for any length of time. As Chloë fidgeted, so Sophie took a cue from her and began fidgeting too. Then she sniffed, several times. When she was bored with that, she belched. I caught her eye, she mistook my glance for amusement and started a stifled giggle behind her hand. She'll fart in a minute, I thought, and even as the thought passed through my mind, so did Sophie's wind pass. She giggled out loud. After a stern look from Chloë, she settled down again, only to draw attention to herself by sighing. I caught Chloë's glance once or twice and her eyes were dancing when she was not rolling them in mock disgust.

Suddenly, something was happening. People were speaking, praying. Sophie was instantly alert. Out of the silence, a woman would drop a thought for us all to consider, then suggest that we pray. Their concerns were both global and personal. After four such contributions Sophie made one.

'I want to pray that my mum finds a friend soon because I know she's lonely,' said Sophie.

A ripple went round the room. Everyone smiled and looked at Sophie, who seemed mighty pleased with herself. Chloë was biting her lip, faintly embarrassed but more pleased than anything, and hugged Sophie.

After the meditation and prayers were over, everyone moved around. Cups of tea appeared. Women asked us who we were, how we had heard of the group. Sister Angela took our names and addresses and asked us if we were interested in meditation.

'I am, a bit,' I said.

'Not really,' said Chloë. 'I came here looking for help, really. I want my daughter to live with me, not her father. She feels the same. Yet he's got her. He kept her after an access visit. I don't stand an eathly if I go to court. I thought the church might help.'

Sister Angela looked apologetic. 'We are not an activist group. Our emphasis is mainly prayer and meditation. There is another group, though that might interest you, and perhaps help you. They are much more, er, militant.'

'That sounds like me,' said Chloë briskly. I felt sorry for Sister Angela, being dismissed so quickly. Chloë wrote down the name and telephone number of the other group. It was called the Guild of Saints Martha and Mary.

'Ruth and Naomi,' I mused later as we returned to Chloë's, 'maybe, but Martha and Mary? They were sisters!'

'All women are sisters!' Chloë retorted. 'And it sounds like a good group. That,' she jerked her head backwards over her shoulder, 'is OK, but there are people who want to speak out . . .'

Sophie interrupted with a wail. 'And I'm one!' she said,

bursting into tears. 'I want to speak out. I heard what you said to that nun. I don't want to go back to Daddy tonight. I want to live with you.'

I found myself making a pot of tea in Chloë's kitchen while she consoled a nearly hysterical Sophie.

'This is what we'll do,' Chloë announced as I poured out the tea for them. 'I'll phone Daddy and say you won't be going back with him. Then I'll phone my solicitor in the morning. Daff, I'm afraid I can't give you a lift home tonight. I'd rather stay put indoors. But if you'd like to stay a while longer, or even overnight, you'll be very welcome. The bed in Auntie's room is made up.'

'A crisis,' I said, 'I haven't had a crisis for ages. I'd be honoured to share yours.'

Sophie's Daddy was due to collect her at seven o'clock. At half past six, Chloë made a brief phone call informing him that she intended to keep Sophie. Strong words from him were met with a cool response. Chloë put the telephone down.

'Honestly,' she muttered, out of Sophie's hearing, 'this child is being treated like a tennis ball. I brought her here with me when I first left. He kept her after Christmas. If I keep her now, he's likely to take me to court. I'm supposed to be an unfit mother, even though he's had a string of housekeepers and babysitters to look after her.'

I made sympathetic noises even though I did not quite understand. It all seemed simple enough to me. If Sophie wanted to live with her mother, then let her.

The phone rang again fifteen minutes later. Daddy, Chloë reported, was worried about his little girl and was coming to fetch her.

'Over my dead body,' said Chloë, drawing the thick velvet curtains with fury.

'I'm not going!' wailed Sophie, loving it all.

'We'll lock the doors and turn out the lights,' said Chloë, 'not a word from you, Sophie, mind, not a snivel.'

Sophie promised and snuggled up to Chloë on the sofa. We all sat in the dark, me in rigid terror, Sophie acting the drama queen and Chloë totally in charge, cold and angry.

He was late. Chloë whispered that he always was. It was at ten past seven that footsteps strode forcefully up the path to the front door. The bell was pushed, but a pretty chime did not convey strength. He lifted the door knocker just once and let it fall, heavily. I jumped. The cat scuttled to the door and mewed to be let out. The bell and the knocker were deployed again. And again. The tension was unbearable. I began to wish I had gone home alone. All sorts of possibilities played on my imagination. Suppose . . .

He banged on the door knocker repeatedly. I heard Sophie whisper, 'I'm frightened.'

Then he walked away. I sighed in relief until I realized that he was standing by the window, trying to peer in. Chloë's thick curtains, however, had left not the slightest chink. He went back to the door and began banging the knocker again. He shouted through the letter-box.

'Sophie! Sophie! I know you're in there. Are you all right?'

I heard a whispered conference between Chloë and Sophie.

'Sophie! It's only your daddy. Are you all right?'

Sophie slid off Chloë's lap and crept to the door. It creaked as she opened it. She nearly tripped over the cat as it shot into the hall. The hall glowed orange from the street lamp shining through the glass of the front door, and spilled into the room we were in. Sophie hung on to the door handle.

'Yes, I'm all right. I want to stay here,' she called.

'Your daddy was worried about you,' came the reply. 'I thought you were happy with Daddy?'

'Your place is boring,' Sophie said.

There was no answer to that. He did not attempt to provide one. We heard footsteps leave the house, the car start up and move away. We laughed as suspense lifted. Sophie went dancing up to her mother, jubilant. Chloë resisted her embrace.

'This time,' she said, wagging her finger in her daughter's face, 'you settle down and stay here even if you *don't* like it. You're nothing but a spoilt brat. When you're eleven, I'm sending you to the strictest convent school I can find. Now, go to bed.'

'Oh! Mum!' wailed Sophie, but Chloë had had enough. When Sophie was safely upstairs, she turned to me.

'They say children of broken marriages suffer! Suffer! This one has had a whale of a time, playing us off, one against the other. Now she's here, she stays. Thanks for your support, Daff. I couldn't have done it if you hadn't been here.'

I gulped. I had been totally unaware of my responsibility for this drama. I slept uneasily in Chloë's aunt's room and my unease was not entirely due to the bed. No wonder, I thought, as I tossed and turned on the lumpy mattress, she spends so much time abroad.

'Jesus, Mary and Joseph!' said Pat when I told him, over lunch the next day, of my exploits at the weekend. I thought he was surprised at the hassle over Sophie, but no, it was the Guild of Saints Martha and Mary that amazed him.

'I thought Martha and Mary, in the gospel story, were sisters.'

'All women are sisters,' I replied.

'You've been talking to Chloë Bidgood,' he said, shaking with laughter, but I failed to see the joke.

'So who have you been talking to?' I said.

'Some guy from Quandary, named Roger. Nice guy,' Pat added casually. 'Says he knows you. I was telling him a bit about you. I hope you don't mind.'

'It depends,' I said darkly, into my bitter lemon, 'what you told him.'

'Only about Bobby.'

'Bobby?'

'Yes. About the book he brought to your sister's wedding.'

'I see. You wish to make a laughing stock of the Mulligan family. Bobby turning up at my sister's wedding, carrying a book on marriage annulment is not something I wish to be known for.'

'I don't blame you,' said Pat, comfortingly. 'But the whole point of the conversation was this. Roger says that you can get your marriage annulled. You have a case. *He* was married. He *knows*, does Roger. Being as you are, you could be seen to be incapable of making a marriage.'

'Oh!' I said, daylight dawning. 'I see! Then poor old Bobby can be a monk in peace?'

'It's the least you can do for the bloke,' said Pat, 'it's a pity you didn't borrow that book of his.'

'I can get it from the library,' I said. The public library was still my means of self-education.

'Isn't Sophie a lovely child?' said Pat changing the subject.

'Lovely!' I repeated. 'She's spoilt, she's precocious, she's demanding.'

'Yes, but she's lovely with it,' Pat insisted.

I had planned to go to the library as soon as I arrived home that evening, but to my surprise Chloë and Sophie were waiting on the doorstep. Not exactly on the doorstep, but, as soon as I was in, my doorbell rang. They must have been waiting down the road, in the car.

Chloë was as near to panic as I had ever seen her.

'We're seeking refuge,' she said, 'and I've come to tell you about the Guild of Saints Martha and Mary.'

'Refuge?' I said, really wanting to know about the guild.

'Yes. I spoke to my solicitor. He,' (meaning her husband, whom she always referred to thus) 'can get an injunction served on me within twenty-four hours. I think twenty-four hours is nearly up. We've been out of the house since I found out. *She,*' lowering her voice and nodding towards Sophie, who was making a nice mess with my talcum powder on the top of my chest of drawers, 'hasn't a clue what it all means. Sophie! leave things alone.'

'Look,' I said, 'I was just going over to the library to get that book and try to sort out my marital problems. I shall have to go now because they close at seven. Do you want to come with me, or shall I make you some coffee and leave you here?'

'Oh, we'll come with you,' said Chloë. 'I'll tell you what I found out about the Saints Martha and Mary lot.'

I was only half-listening as she talked about the group meeting in someone's flat, the next meeting being after Easter. I was wondering if I would be able to find the book in the library. Probably I would have to order it. Would it be quicker to write to Bobby and ask to borrow his copy? It all depended on the speed with which he replied.

Sophie ran off to inspect the children's library. I had a quick look for *Marriage Annulment* on the shelves but could not find it, so went to the desk and inquired. I had to fill in a reservation card. When I turned round, Chloë had gone. Sophie appeared.

'Mum said would you keep an eye on me,' said Sophie.

'Where is she? Where's your mum?' I said in mild panic.

Suppose Sophie's father found her while she was in my unwilling charge?

'She's gone to the loo,' Sophie said.

'Oh,' I said. 'But they won't let her use the loo here.'

'Do you like my mum?' Sophie asked. Her voice carried remarkably. It was far too loud for a library.

'Yes, she's quite nice,' I whispered.

'Cos she likes you,' Sophie went on.

'Sophie! Daff!' Chloë appeared behind us, distressed. 'Aren't there any loos in this part of London . . .'

'Here,' I said, handing over my keys, 'run back to my

place. I'll follow with Sophie.'

Chloë gasped her thanks and fled. I filled in my library request card and left, Sophie holding my hand with a touching, but quite unjustified, trust, after inspecting an exhibition of paintings on my way out. It was nudity, not art, which appealed to Sohpie.

The front door had been left on the latch, so I closed it behind us. The door of my room was open too. I could hear Chloë, by now happier, talking to someone, and the sound of cups and spoons being set out.

'Who's that lady?' Sophie asked as she pushed the door open wider.

My face dropped. Chloë was, on my behalf, entertaining a visitor who perched tensely on the edge of my bed, snivelling into an inadequate tissue and brushing tears away as they rolled down the front of her fake-fur coat.

'Oh Daff!' said Chloë.

'Daffodil!' said the visitor.

'Mother!' I gasped.

'Mum . . .' began Sophie, knowing she had been upstaged.

I closed the door. Chloë winked at me and made some coffee. Mother burst into loud sobs. Sophie looked round wildly for something to do while the adults were preoccupied.

'Your mother was on the doorstep when I arrived,' Chloë explained, 'so I made her welcome in your absence.'

It was just as well Chloë had been welcoming for I wasn't.

'What on earth are you doing here, Mother?' I demanded.

Mother sighed and moaned then mumbled into the soggy tissue. 'I've left your father.'

'You've done what?' There was a long pause while I absorbed this information. Then I said, more calmly, eyeing the suit-case I now spied on the floor. 'Don't be ridiculous, Mother. You can't do a thing like that.'

Mother looked at me sideways, over the balled up tissue.

'You did,' she said.

A sudden movement from Chloë's direction gave me the distinct impression that she was laughing.

'Yes,' I said carefully, 'I left Bobby. I had a very good reason. Have you got a reason?'

'Yes, I'm tired of it all. I'm tired of the routine, I'm tired of him and his smelly feet, I'm tired of washing his socks.'

How did one deal with an errant mother? I had no idea. On errant daughters, I was an expert. I could tell anyone how they should be handled.

'What did you plan to do?' I asked.

'I was going to ask you if I could stay here,' Mother said, looking round the room. 'But you don't have anywhere to put me.'

'No, thank goodness,' I said rudely. 'I know what you're playing at.'

Mother would have given me a dirty look, but Chloë was watching her. She tried looking pathetic instead as Chloë helped her off with her fake-fur coat.

CHAPTER 19

Chloë calmed the atmosphere. 'Daff will be pleased that you understand how she left Bobby, Mrs Mulligan. I only wish that my mother had understood me.'

'My mother never understood me,' said Mother.

'Do you understand me, Mum?' asked Sophie.

'Of course I do, dear,' said Chloë 'only too well!'

Sophie beamed. Mother tilted her head and smiled touchingly at Sophie. Mother felt in her handbag and gave Sophie some sweets, which Sophie accepted with well-rehearsed grace. Mother was captivated. What a nice child, I guessed she was thinking. Daffodil was never so well-mannered at this age. Chloë winked at me again. My legs went to jelly. I went to pieces. I watched fascinated as Chloë charmed my Mother, made her talk, sympathized, made tactful suggestions. I gazed at Chloë's soft blue eyes. They sometimes met my gaze at first in surprise, then amusement, then in a way that added to my resentment at Mother's intrusion. I waited for a repetition of the conspiratorial wink. I wanted to return the next one. I let the conversation flow over me as I watched Chloë. Mother was relaxed and smiling, even laughing. I was impatient for her to leave. I was not concerned about where she should go. And Sophie. Perhaps Mother and Sophie could be despatched together.

They certainly seemed to be getting on well. Mother was smiling and feeding Sophie sweets. Perhaps they could go round to the off-licence together. By now, I had totally lost the thread of the conversation.

'You're so understanding,' Mother cooed at Chloë. 'Daffodil could learn so much from you.'

This amused Chloë. She replied by defending me.

'Daffodil had had a difficult time.'

Mother looked at me.

'Poor Daffodil,' she sighed. Blaming not sympathizing.

That was it. I could control myself no longer.

'I know what game you're playing, Mother,' I said. 'And I'm not letting you play it. You couldn't make me like you, so now you want to be like me! Go back to Daddy!'

'Ssh!' said Chloë.

'I am! I am!,' said Mother. 'Your friend has kindly offered to drive me to the station. I'm going back to think things over. There's no need to show yourself up in front of your friend.'

'Mum!' said Sophie, 'I'm going to be sick.'

'Poor little girl,' said Mother, taking her hand. 'Where's the bathroom?'

My mother and Chloë's daughter left the room. There was a brief, still pause between me and Chloë. Then we spoke together.

'Daff!' she said.

'Chloë!' I said.

This was the moment I had been waiting for and it seemed that Chloë had been waiting for it, too.

There was a noise from the direction of the bathroom. We both froze. The noise came again; it sounded like a shaking and banging on the door.

'Mum!' shouted Sophie. 'Mum!'

'Yes?' called Chloë, not moving.

'Mum! We're locked in the bathroom. We can't get out!

And I've been sick.'

Mother's refined tones called 'Daffodil! Daffodil!'

Chloë grinned.

I grinned.

'Hang on,' I called back, 'We're caught up for a minute.'

And we were.